# CHRISTMAS COVE

## SARAH DRESSLER

5 PRINCE PUBLISHING

Published by 5 PRINCE PUBLISHING & BOOKS, LLC

PO Box 865, Arvada, CO 80001

www.5PrinceBooks.com

ISBN digital: 978-1-63112-340-5

ISBN print: 978-1-63112-341-2

Cover Credit: Marianne Nowicki

09122023

*This book is dedicated to all the people who have found their Christmas in the most unexpected of places, and to my family for sharing in the adventure.*

# ACKNOWLEDGMENTS

I'd like to thank my husband for being my biggest
cheerleader.

My children, who listen to all my story ideas,
and for whom I added the squirrel friend to America's
journey.

A gigantic thank you to Jaimie, for encouraging me to start
in the first place.

To my fantastic team, from my beta readers on up,
for bringing this book to the world.

To all my readers,
I appreciate each and every one of you.

# CHRISTMAS COVE

# CHAPTER 1

A PIECE OF GOLDEN BREAD POPPED FROM THE TOASTER. WITH A small white plate in one hand, America twirled through her kitchen. Plucking the warm toast from its cage, she placed it all on the counter. From the butter dish to the knife drawer, and to the fridge where she retrieved her favorite strawberry jam, dancing around her morning routine left her feeling prepared to take on the day.

Checking the time, she noticed that she was slightly behind schedule and was still wearing her red plaid pajamas. Nothing peeved America more than running behind. *If you're not early, you're late*, she told herself as her teeth crunched into her breakfast.

She swiped her finger across her phone's home screen and opened the weather app. *Another warm day*, she thought. With Christmas two weeks away, she had yet to see a single flurry, and disappointment wrinkled her nose.

*Of all the years to have a warm December!* Her parents were going out of town this year, and she would miss enjoying her favorite winter activities with them. She loved skating in the snow at the outdoor rink with her father, and she would miss the annual Christmas Eve Santa Hunt that one of the local neighborhoods hosts each year. America supposed she could go alone, but cringed at the idea.

"Oh, drat!" America remembered that her parents were leaving . . . today.

She brushed the crumbs from her fingertips before swiping her phone to the video chat app. Her momentary panic at having missed saying goodbye to her parents before their flight dissipated when her mother answered after only one ring.

"I was wondering if you were going to give me a call," her mother said.

"Is that America?" her father asked from somewhere off the screen.

America motioned with a flick of her hand. "Is Dad there? I can hear him, but I can't see him."

Her mother panned the phone around. Dozens of people hurried around in the background with their luggage and children in tow. Loud, overhead announcements screeched through the receiver. To one side, the bright morning sun streamed through a wall of windows and glared across her mother's face.

"Mom," America said. "Mom! You're making me dizzy."

"Oh. Sorry, dear. Here he is," her mom said. "Can you see us both now?"

The video tornado stopped, and the announcements ended, allowing America room to speak. "I'm going to miss you both so much," she said. "Even though your favorite daughter can't go with you, I'm sure you're going to have a wonderful adventure in Italy."

Her parents hadn't invited her, not that she could have gone anyway with all the work needed to wrap up the magazine's end-of-year issue. But her parents beamed. They had waited a lifetime to take this trip, and America was glad that her mom and dad could experience it together.

"Don't be glum," her dad said. "We'll be back in a couple of weeks. And just in time for Christmas."

Her mom shifted the view onto her face alone. "You'll have extra time while we're away to work on your writing. Or maybe go on a date—"

"Mom!"

"Who's that nice man you spoke about who works with you at the magazine? What about him?"

America felt her eyes roll and wished her father would interrupt again. "I don't need to date anyone. And besides, I'm going to be super busy at work and I'm sure I won't even notice the time flying by," she lied. If there was anything she *would* notice, it was time.

"Honey, you haven't been out with anyone new since your breakup with Alan a few months ago."

America knew her mother meant well. Alan had been a great boyfriend, until he wasn't. It was during a short trip to the shore when she realized he was more interested in taking selfies and working on his tan than he was in spending time with her or even thinking about anyone other than himself. She had broken it off without delay, deciding that no amount of fun was worth staying with such a selfish person.

"I know you want me to be happy, and I love you for it. But I'm sure I'll enjoy Christmas with or without a man in my life." America giggled at her father in the background of the video pointing at himself. She would always have a wonderful man to look up to in her dad. "Plus, did you see the weather? It's going to be warm for at least the next few days. What kind of Christmas is it with shorts, and tank tops, and flip-flops—"

"How do you think they celebrate in the southern hemisphere?" her dad interjected. "It's summer in Australia right now. I bet they still put out trees and snowmen, even those cute lighted reindeer in their front yards. And do you know what? I doubt they whine about the weather."

"So, you hung up your ties at the law firm and now you're some kind of meteorologist?" America joked, even though he was probably right. "Be that as it may, it just doesn't feel right without snow. Or even a coat and scarf, for that matter."

"Or someone to kiss under the mistletoe." Her mother's eyebrows raised in rapid succession. "Please try to have a little fun. It'll turn cold soon enough, just you wait. And perhaps you'll have someone by then to help keep you warm," her mom said and rubbed the tip of her nose against her dad's. "We plan on enjoying ourselves, too."

"Gross," America said as an announcement squawked through the airport's loudspeakers, causing her to check the time once more. "I'm going to be late for work. I have to get going," she said. "I love you both."

"Love you too," her mom said. "Promise me you'll at least try and have a good couple of weeks."

America nodded and blew her mom a kiss through the screen. "Have a safe flight."

The screen darkened, and America darted to the bedroom where her blush pink blouse and black cigarette pants waited for her at the end of the bed. She slipped on her clothes and ran a brush through the curls in her hair that she had set before breakfast. She grabbed her phone off the kitchen counter and dropped it in her purse. At the door, she flipped the light switch off and watched as the flocked Christmas tree in the corner dimmed. In her estimation, there was nothing sadder than an unlit Christmas tree.

In the elevator, America fought the urge to check her watch again, knowing full well that she was still on time. She looked at the wood ceiling panels and counted the numbered buttons on the wall panel indicating the building's floors.

The numbers ticked down from seven, and the lift slowed down as it approached floor three. The doors slid open and an all-too-familiar face greeted her with the side-eye that seemed permanently etched on her landlady's face.

"Morning, Ms. Meadows," America said and scooched to one side of the elevator.

"Is it? I hadn't noticed." The older woman shrugged and buried her nose in the pages of a book titled, *Gen-Z for Dummies*.

America sucked in a giggle and held it until the elevator hit the ground floor. "Have a lovely day. And Merry Christmas," she said to her landlady on the way out through the lobby.

Like a million little Christmas lights, crystal sun rays scattered geometric reflections from the building's windows onto the opposite side of the street. A neighbor she recognized, but didn't know, entered the door and held it open for her. A scent of fresh cinnamon rolls hit her nose. The man carried a whole box full in one hand, which reminded her of the order of delicious treats waiting for her at the bakery down the street.

"Thank you," America said to the gentleman. "And Merry Christmas."

Though the weather forecast called for warmer temperatures later in the day, the morning air was still crisp, and the harsh sounds of an awakening city welcomed her outside as she descended the stone steps to street level. She turned right and stopped at the corner where a stone bench encircled a naked maple tree. Its leaves had fallen weeks earlier, having apparently missed the memo on the unusual late-year heatwave.

Up in the branches, a furry friend flicked its bushy tail. America dropped a handful of nuts on the top edge of the bench-back as she walked by. Typically, America would stand by and watch the critter spiral down the tree trunk to collect the prize. But today, she had no time, and settled for a smart, "You're welcome," as she continued on her way to the bakery.

"Morning, America," the man behind the counter said. "I nearly thought you had forgotten about your order. But it's all ready for you."

America noted the time. Late or not, these holiday treats were well worth any delay. She opened the slim cardboard box and inhaled the sweet smell of pastries glistening with sugar and spices. Christmas was the perfect excuse to spoil her coworkers. *Who doesn't like treats?* she thought.

"This is great," she said and closed the box. "Thank you, Frank. And Merry Christmas." America flew through the door with her box of holiday pastries in hand and hastened down the street towards her office.

From sidewalk to sky, America's eyes followed the cut lines of gray stones up her building's front façade. A polished black sign hanging above the golden framed glass doors read Chadwick House Publishing. At the stately doors, a porter ushered her through to the lobby, where dozens of people gathered.

Up ten floors, the elevator doors slid open, and she stepped into the sun-washed office spaces of Jet Trek Online Magazine, the hottest travel site in the country. Partitions of glass, framed in black steel, allowed light to filter effortlessly through the room. Bookcases overflowed with resources and paper archives of the digital magazine's editions from over the years. Jet Trek had ninety-six, to be exact. *But who's counting?* she thought.

It was America who was counting. As the magazine's editor, it was part of her job to know everything pertaining to all the previous issues. There was software she could use to cross reference and check any works in the archive, but there was nothing quite like the scent of old paper stock, slowly aging like a fine wine and filled like a time capsule with memories of the past.

She patted a hand on the side of one of the bookcases as she walked through to where her office waited for her in the far corner. Poppy, America's assistant, leaned out from behind her own computer and a wide grin spread across her face.

"What do we have here?" Poppy said and shot out of her seat, taking the box of pastries from America's hand.

On cue, and as though called by a dog whistle, coworkers appeared out of the recesses and converged on the treats.

All their smiling faces and merry salutations filled America's heart. But there was someone missing, someone she could always count on to come and snag a pastry *and give her a smoldering glance.* America peered to the left down a long corridor and saw him. In her mind's eye, a marquee blinked in bright Broadway-style bulbs: *Mark Moore, Lead Travel Writer,* floating in the air above his perfectly tousled salt-and-pepper head as he ambled towards her.

Mark was the kind of writer America hoped herself to be someday. Since coming to the magazine five years ago, she had stayed in her current comfortable position, and there was no one to blame but herself. She was simply a great editor, and she was no "Mark Moore". Mark's confident yet approachable style contributed to the magazine's success in recent years and made him a legend in the industry.

On America's first day of work, and before she knew who he was, she had found Mark sitting in her office, to *get some peace.* She had disturbed that peace when she announced that he was sitting in *her* chair and at *her* desk. After the awkward interaction, she preferred communicating with him via email and through Poppy. America didn't know if she was intimidated more by his status, or by her physical attraction to him. Either way, she was a statue around Mark.

"Good morning, America," Mark said, smoldering glance and all.

She stood, slack-jawed, words having departed her mind. A sharp elbow jabbed her in the ribs, and she shook the fog away.

"May I?" he asked and tilted his head to the box of holiday treats.

She nodded.

"Are you in town for the holidays?" Poppy asked Mark in a sweet effort to break the tension.

"No. Just passing through and had to drop some ideas with Janowitz. I don't really do . . ." Mark put his hands up and seemed to be washing away his surroundings, " . . . all this holiday stuff. Pastries excluded, of course."

If America could speak, she would have convinced him that Christmas is simply the best, most magical time of the year. All this *Christmas stuff* is worth every penny and every ounce of energy because it makes others happy and full of joy. But as it was, her mouth ceased operations in his presence. She smiled, and he probably thought she agreed with his absurd point of view.

Mark turned with his frosted, Santa-shaped cookie in hand and shook it in the air as he walked away. "Thanks for the cookie, America."

America grunted and slapped her palm to her forehead.

"What is the matter with you?" Poppy asked and stood in America's line of sight.

"I don't know whether to be offended that he doesn't like Christmas, or to start writing, *America Moore*, in my Lisa Frank notebook."

"You've got it bad," Poppy laughed.

"I've got something, that's for certain."

# CHAPTER 2

ONE BY ONE, HER COWORKERS CLAIMED THE HOLIDAY TREATS and exchanged pleasantries. Bringing a bit of joy and indulgence was the least she could do for the people who worked alongside her each day to make the magazine successful. Once the crowd thinned, America motioned for Poppy to follow her to her desk, where they could speak in relative quiet.

America hung her purse on a coat tree. "What's on the schedule for today?"

Poppy's brows pinched together. "You've got a meeting," she said, "with Mr. Janowitz."

America felt her heart drop in her chest, and she rubbed her throat where it constricted. It was the same feeling she had whenever she was called into the principal's office back in high school.

"What does he want?" America asked as she sucked a deep breath into her belly.

"Not sure," Poppy said and checked the time. "Wow! Staring at Mark and eating cookies took longer than I thought. You've got about ten minutes to get up there. You know he doesn't tolerate tardiness."

"Nor do I." America fidgeted with a rogue curl across her forehead. "Do I look all right?"

"Perfect, like always," Poppy said and turned America towards the door. "Now go."

America didn't know what she would do without Poppy. Not a writer or an editor, Poppy was great with time and people. She kept everything running smoothly so that America could get her work done in the most effective way and in the least amount of time. Which reminded her . . .

"Did you send my edits on the Croatia package?" America asked as she walked towards the elevator. "And did we get the approval for that restaurant reviewer? What was her name?"

"Yes, to Croatia. And yes, to Miska, the reviewer." The phone at Poppy's desk rang, interrupting her answer. Poppy threw a finger up and rushed over to her workspace, while America waited to see if her meeting with Janowitz was canceled.

Poppy picked up the phone and answered in her usual professional manner. After a short exchange, Poppy covered the receiver with her palm. "It's your landlady. She says it's urgent."

"Take a message," America instructed.

Poppy nodded and put the landlady on hold. "Everything is under control. Go!"

America steeled herself for whatever was coming from the boss, Janowitz, who waited in his office on the eleventh floor. She combed her brain for any reason he would want to see her. There was nothing she had done to warrant such a meeting. Nothing bad, anyway. It was possible that he wished to see her in person to give her a holiday bonus.

Though he had never given bonuses in person any other year, it was a nice thought.

In the mirror reflection inside the lift, she plastered a smooth and confident grin on her face. Then the doors opened to a sparsely decorated vestibule, and she felt her smile deflate. Two black couches flanked a marble coffee table, where a vase held olive branches and pine sprigs. It was as festive as Mr. Janowitz was with his holiday decorations but was better than none at all.

Through the paned glass wall, America waved at her boss, who was speaking on the phone. A stressed red flushed his face. He slammed the phone down as he stood from his seat and paced around the long side of his desk before making his way to the door.

"Come on in, America," he said and motioned for her to enter.

America trotted over, her high heels tapping against the white terrazzo floor and echoing in her ears. It was difficult to discern whether the noise was from her stilettos or from her own heartbeat pounding in her head. She turned and closed the door, even though there was no one else around to hear them. The lines on her boss's forehead indicated a serious conversation was coming her way.

"Thank you for seeing me on such short notice," he said and plonked down into his cognac leather desk chair. "I trust you are having a pleasant holiday season?"

America nodded. "I am," she said and noticed her boss swivel back and forth in his seat. "But I don't think you asked me here to discuss Christmas."

"On the contrary. Christmas is the exact reason I asked you here today."

"Curious," America said and relaxed into her own chair across from him. "If there's one thing that I love to talk about more than anything else at this time of year, it's the holidays. What's on your mind?"

"You love Christmas," he said, "and I have a problem."

He was beating around the holly bush for an unknown reason. "Whatever your Christmas dilemma, I'm sure I can help. What is it? Gift ideas? Decorating? Because I see your pine arrangement out there, and I think we can do a bit better than that, don't you?"

Mr. Janowitz leaned over and peered over America's shoulder into the vestibule. "What's wrong with my pine twigs?"

"Oh. Nothing. They're great. Very festive. All I meant was —"

"Relax, America. I didn't call you up here for any decorating advice."

"You didn't?" Tension returned to her neck just as quickly as it had gone a moment earlier.

"I have an assignment for you, and I need it done before the Christmas Eve issue goes live online," he said and typed something into his keyboard.

"Of course. I can move other projects off by a week or two that aren't due until after the new year."

"Great. I need you to pack your bags."

"Bags? Sir, I don't understand."

"The thing is, Meghan is sick, and she was supposed to be on her way to cover this story as we speak. I've gone over all my options. All my other writers are either on assignment already this week, or aren't as good a fit for this type of story as you are."

"But . . . I'm not a writer. I edit things. I sit at my desk and study data and trends, and curate the reader's experience. I don't . . . travel," America said. "Isn't there someone else?"

He turned his computer around and pointed to the screen splashed with wintery images. America imagined herself walking the picturesque town lane lined with snow-flocked trees and twinkling lights. On the corner, a Santa rings a bell. Large snowflakes fall around her. She looks up to the sky, sticks out her tongue, and tastes winter's lace. Magic sparks in her mind and pulls at her heart.

"Listen," Mr. Janowitz said, and shook her from her daydream. "I know this would be your first article, but I believe you are up to the challenge. I've read your reports and edited articles for how many years now?"

"Five."

"For five years," he said, as though he had known the correct answer all along. "You're fantastic—"

"And you have no one else," she finished. "I'm sorry. But I don't think I can do it."

"You're right. I'm out of options, okay? But the truth is, I need you. I'm begging you. Please take this article," he said.

"But it's Christmas," America's voice sounded whinier than she meant. "I have plans to enjoy the city here. The Santa Hunt, ice skating, the Christmas market . . ."

"Christmas. Exactly. The assignment is simple. I need you to go and report on a town known for its Christmas traditions. Look at this." Mr. Janowitz clicked through images on the screen of tree lighting festivals, Christmas markets, children skating on a lake, and a bonfire. "You'll have all the Christmas you can contend with on this assignment."

Intrigued, she scanned the computer images. As much as she yearned for an exciting holiday season, there was one small fact that she couldn't wrap her mind around. "But sir, I'm not a writer."

He turned his computer back around. "Just think about it like writing up one of your reports. If you write the basic story, I can have one of the other writers review it. It'll be fun, and you have nothing to lose."

"I just don't know whether I'm the right person."

"I'll double your pay and cover all your expenses. I'll even take care of your cat," he said.

"I don't have a cat, but I appreciate the sentiment." America stood and crossed her arms. "I can't take the assignment. I'm not a writer, and . . ." She would need to think up a better excuse, because the more she said it, the sillier it sounded to her.

"I realize this is last minute. Will you at least consider going? Just let me know by . . . noon? That way, I can get back to the mayor and let him know that I'm not sending anyone out."

"The mayor requested the feature?" she asked.

"That's right. He made it sound so good and, correct me if I'm wrong, the magazine hasn't featured a Christmas town in a long time."

"No, it's been years." America walked four steps to the door and opened the heavy glass panel. The fragrant pine branches in the vase seemed to smile at her, and she said, "I'll think about it."

# CHAPTER 3

THE LIFT DOORS OPENED TO THE SIGHT OF POPPY'S BRIGHT smile. "Well? What was all that about?" she asked.

"Let's walk," America said and made for her office. She trained her eyes on the polished floor and avoided any unnecessary conversations on her way. "Do I look as stunned as I feel?"

Poppy skipped ahead and halted America. "Let's see here," she said. With her hands, she manually straightened America's shoulders and brushed non-existent dust from her sleeves. "You look completely normal. Should I be worried?"

Satisfied with Poppy's inspection, America pushed past her. The shock of Mr. Janowitz's request had by no means worn off, but she was able to walk the remaining steps to her small corner office, where she fell into a plush pink chair and rested her feet on the edge of the desk.

Poppy closed the glass door and sat across from America in a matching seat. "Spill," she said.

"Janowitz wants me to draft an article. For the current issue. That's only a few days away."

Poppy clapped her hands together. "That's fantastic. You're a good writer?"

"I mean . . ." America threw her head back. "I'm an editor, yes, but I don't draft original content. Even if I did, there's no way I can give him what he wants in such a short timeframe."

"Well, what's the assignment, his expectations?"

"He's in a pickle. Meghan called out at the last minute, and no other writers were available to go to some little Christmas town. He said I can turn in a very rough draft, and he'll get one of the other staff writers to help shape it."

"That sounds easy enough for a first assignment. Why are you flustered about it?" Poppy handed her a candy cane across the desk. "Here, the peppermint will help calm you."

Taking the candy in hand, America unwrapped the cane's stick end and tapped it on her lower lip. "You know these things don't have real peppermint in them."

"Just eat it," Poppy said and unwrapped a candy cane of her own. "Has anyone ever told you how stubborn you are?"

"Once or twice," she said. Of course, America had heard the accusation before, but she disagreed with the sentiment. She preferred to see herself as determined rather than stubborn. Stubborn implied an unmoving state of being. Determination—er—persistence was the hallmark characteristic of a successful editor.

"So, why the sad face?" Poppy asked.

"I suppose I wasn't expecting anything like this when I woke up today. Decorating his office or helping with his gift list would have been a fruitcake-walk compared to what he wants me to do." She sucked the candy for a moment as she considered the opportunity. "On the other hand, I know I would have never asked for this assignment, and it might be nice to go do some festive activities. Apparently, their traditions are a big deal."

"What's it called?" Poppy asked.

Janowitz never did say, but America recalled the name from the images on her boss's computer screen. "Christmas Cove."

"No wonder he asked you to do it. You love the holidays."

"I don't think I'm going to do it," America said, though a legitimate reason escaped her as she prepared her inevitable rebuttal to whatever Poppy would say next.

"Why not?" Poppy said and slapped her hand on the desktop. "You love Christmas, and the place is called Christmas Cove, for goodness' sake!"

"I don't think I can do it. I don't create original content for the mag. I edit. I pore over trends and data and tell the writers what we need."

"This is no different. You craft emails and proposals and do research already. This is just a next step up, an extension of your natural world, if you will."

"I appreciate the confidence . . . but it's last minute, and —"

"And you have nothing else to do," Poppy interrupted. "I can't make you do it, but the assignment seems like a perfect fit. Not to mention, it won't be hard to exceed Mr. Janowitz's low expectations. It's a fantastic opportunity."

"He needs to know if I'll take the job by noon today."

Poppy looked at the clock, and America realized she hadn't checked her watch in a while. Looking down, she noted the time.

"Sixty-seven minutes," they said in unison, and each laughed.

"I suppose I'd better get to thinking," America said.

"About that," Poppy said. "I spoke with your landlady."

"What does she want?"

"This might make your decision easier. Apparently, there was some sort of water main break at your building, and the city won't have it fixed for at least a week. She said all the residents must evacuate while the problem is being fixed."

"Seriously?" America's forehead fell into her palm, and she massaged the spot beside her eye. That's it. There really was nothing keeping her from going. Her parents were happily in the air on their way to Italy, and now she was going to be out on the street while the city fixed the water problem at her apartment.

Poppy walked towards the door. "I'll just give you a minute. Let me know how I can help."

America tapped a finger on the side of her computer. "Some Christmas this is shaping up to be!" she said and typed Christmas Cove into the search bar.

A photo grid appeared on the display. America easily imagined herself amongst the idyllic, snow-covered pines and dancing below twinkling lights. If she had to spend the next week somewhere other than her home, it looked as good a place as any other.

America poked her head out of the door and knocked on the frame. Poppy looked up from her work with a raised brow. "I'm going home to pack," America said.

"Yes!" Poppy stood and clapped. "I knew you'd be excited to do it."

"Not exactly," America said, "but since I have to find somewhere to stay for a week, it might as well be Christmas Cove."

"Looks like Santa has plans for you this year, after all," Poppy said.

"Oh, stop!" America turned and reached for her bag. "Can you let the boss know?"

"Already done."

"What?"

Poppy shrugged. "I figured you would come around, although not in such a dramatic fashion. So, I made the call."

Poppy handed over a paper. "This is your itinerary. The driver will be at your apartment in an hour."

"You took care of everything. Thank you." America stopped in her apprehensive quicksand. "You really think I can do this?"

Poppy turned America down the walkway. "I know you can. And if you need anything at all—"

"I know." America hugged Poppy and kissed both of her cheeks. "I will call you. Thank you for being my biggest cheerleader."

"Always. Now go."

The elevator doors opened, and America took the first step from her comfortable life as an editor into the unknowns of becoming a writer. "Merry Christmas," she said through the narrow gap as the door shut.

# CHAPTER 4

AMERICA TOOK ONE LAST LOOK AROUND THE APARTMENT. SHE gripped the suitcase handle with an uncommon tightness and all but strangled it in her sweaty palm. A list of all the things she didn't want to forget ran through her head, and she checked each one off.

"Coat? Check. Charger? Check. Computer and notebooks? Yes." As though the completed checklist wasn't enough, she gave herself a pep talk. "You got this, America. It's just a trip in which you get to write notes. No biggie."

With a nod, she walked from her bedroom through the living area and stopped in front of the Christmas tree. She palmed the hammered metal cross from one of the branches and slipped it into the front pocket of the suitcase for good luck. Taking each of her favorites in hand, she felt the glittery texture of the little farmhouse, and the smooth red velvet of the cardinal wearing a sweater. The gold sheen of the starburst ornament glinted in her eye. Her mother had given it to her last year to remind her to always shine brightly.

That was easier said than done on a day like the one she was having. While operating inside her routine, there was little to fear. But the known was now an unknown. As she turned the lights off and closed the door, she shut out the predictable and invited the unfamiliar to join her adventure.

There was no sign of Ms. Meadows, though America would have liked to say goodbye on her way out. She was no doubt busy putting out metaphorical fires with the city workers and other tenants. Unwelcome news always seems worse during the holidays, and America could sympathize with the landlady. The other tenants weren't likely to be as kind as America was about the whole thing. So, she taped a Christmas card on Ms. Meadows's mailbox on her way through the lobby.

Outside, a black SUV waited at the bottom of the stone steps. The driver, recognizing her, opened the door. "Ms. Greene?" he said.

"Yes. Sorry to keep you waiting. I'll be just a moment." America rolled her large gold suitcase to him and handed him a tote bag.

While the driver loaded her luggage, America hurried down the street to the corner, where she spotted her little friend. Jessica, the squirrel, with her curled tail and chubby cheeks, sat atop a lower branch. America took out a handful of nuts and a couple of biscuits and placed them on the bench. Jessica looked on and hesitated before spiraling down the tree towards the loot.

"Merry Christmas," America said and returned to the SUV.

"All ready?" the driver said with a friendly grin.

"As I'll ever be," she said and took his hand as she climbed inside the vehicle. "Thank you."

The driver closed the door and walked around to the driver's seat. "It'll be a couple of hours, but we should arrive by five. There's no weather to account for at this time. If you need anything, you can press the green button on the console in front of you. Otherwise, I'll see you when we get to your destination. Sit back and relax."

The man didn't even take a breath, as though he were a recording. "What's your name? I'm told not to take rides from strangers," she joked.

"Brampson, ma'am."

"Thank you Brampson. Will you let me know when we are getting close? I'd like to take notes on my first impressions."

"Of course," he said, and the privacy partition rose between them.

America sat back and dropped her head to the headrest. "I can't believe I'm doing this," she said aloud, and the car lurched forward. Her trusty watch buzzed the hour on her wrist, and she wondered how her parents' flight was going, and how surprised they were going to be when she told them what she was up to. In her estimation, they were somewhere near the Azores on the way to their layover in Paris.

Her mother said they would call when they got to Italy, and America planned to tell them about her adventure then. And perhaps, by then, she'd have something to tell. Up until that moment, all she had done was pack a bag and feed a squirrel. She would need something a bit more interruption-worthy if she were going to take away any time from her parents' once-in-a-lifetime vacation.

America used the remaining battery life in her computer to look up everything she could about Christmas Cove. She learned that a young entrepreneur founded the town in the year 1869, when the railroad needed a watering station beside the lake. Later, when industry had moved nearby, the picturesque lake setting was the preferred destination for locals to spend any leisure time.

The summer playpen expanded into a winter haven after World War II, when returning soldiers took their families to quiet spots dotted throughout New England for long-awaited holidays. Christmas Cove lived up to its name with one of the biggest festivals in the area: The Bonfire of Fears.

America giggled when she read about it. It sounded worse than it was.

According to the custom, a bonfire is set ablaze on the icy shore, and people write their prayers and their fears on rice paper and throw them into the flames. When the paper incinerates, the tiny particles float skyward with the rising heat.

What a beautiful image the event created in her heart!

The battery icon on America's computer blinked death, and she put it away, opting for an old standard instead, her favorite book.

# CHAPTER 5

"I APPRECIATE YOU COMING OVER TO HELP GET THE PLACE ready," Leo said. "I can't believe that I got such a great booking this time of the year. It was a long shot trying to rent this place out, all things considered."

"It's not like there's much else to do around here," Edwin teased. "You know I'm happy to help you out. Now, where should I start?"

Leo handed the older man two brown grocery bags and pointed at the cabin. He had a few hours until the guest would arrive, and he wanted the place to be perfect. Having a long booking hadn't happened in years, and he was thankful for the chunk of change the travel agency said the guest was willing to pay to stay there.

He hadn't even argued when the name on the booking had switched from Meghan to America. He didn't care much who she was.

Edwin came back out of the cabin and skipped down the front steps. "What's next? Do you want me to go into town and get a few decorations? It is Christmas, after all."

Leo looked out at the vast and empty countryside with

fog lingering in the southern sky and sighed. "I don't think it'll be necessary. But thanks for the offer." Leo handed the man two more bags from the bed of his truck and carried the tub, overflowing with fresh linens, inside.

While Edwin loaded the fridge with fresh produce and drinks, Leo made up the bed with layers of white sheets and a soft duvet. He hated that he knew the name for the thin covering and wished his mother hadn't always been such a stickler for the way beds were supposed to be made. But here he was, about to turn thirty years old, and making up a bed in his little cabin with the most expensive sheets and blankets he'd ever purchased.

"You think she's pretty?" Edwin yelled from the kitchen.

"Who are you talking about? Don't tell me you bought another horse!"

"I'm talking about the lady. The one checking in today."

"Why would I even care? It's a booking. I'm simply happy to have one. Not to mention, if she's a writer, she probably looks like she's been locked up in a bookstore for the better part of her adult life and speaks in poetic soliloquies like she's a long-lost Bennet sister."

"That's a very specific response," Edwin laughed.

Joining Edwin in the kitchen, Leo sorted some of the dry goods on the counter. "It's a habit. My mother was a literature teacher."

"All I'm saying is to keep your mind and eyes open. You never know when a chance will be your only chance."

"Now that sounds like a very specific response too," Leo pointed out. "Are you speaking from experience?"

"I'm nearly seventy years old, of course I'm speaking from experience." Edwin shut the fridge door and gathered the trash into one of the emptied brown paper bags. "When was the last time you dated? I know there are no unmarried women in town that are age-appropriate for you. Unless you count Scrooge McCarol."

"Pa!" Leo scolded, using Edwin's nickname. "Carol is your age, first of all. Secondly, I don't need to go on dates to find someone. I'll just know her when I see her."

"And you'll never find her if you don't go anywhere outside this town of yours," Edwin said. "But I, for one, feel like something big is about to happen for you. For this town. You know what I mean?"

Leo stopped his tidying and looked around the space. Creamy linen drapes hung loosely at the windows and framed the gray of autumn holding tightly to the structures outside. Birch logs stacked perfectly in the fireplace all screamed home to him. With the newly made-up bed and food stocked in the kitchen, the cabin's energy was more cozy than exciting.

"Nope. Pa, I don't feel it. This place feels the same as it always has." Leo patted Edwin on the shoulders. "Whoever she is, I hope she has a nice stay here, and that's it."

"And maybe tell all her fancy city friends to book their own stay here, too?"

"Now, wouldn't that be a miracle?" Leo said as he shut off the lights and locked up the cabin door until later.

# CHAPTER 6

THE WORLD OF ELIZABETH BENNET WRAPPED AMERICA IN ITS romance and thought-provoking humor so completely that time seemed to stand still inside the vehicle. No matter how often America read the classic story, she always felt like a scene was missing. The Bennet family never experiences Christmas together, at least not that the reader sees.

America imagined a holiday moment, with all the sisters vying for their father's approval in their varied ways. Mary playing Christmas hymns on the pianoforte and Lizzy burying her nose in a book while secretly making fun of her family's ridiculousness. As an only child, America had always wished to be part of something as grand as Regency-era England, save for the lack of indoor plumbing and inaccurate timepieces.

She lifted her wrist and checked the time on her smartwatch. Hours had passed. Out the window, tree-lined fields and granite-topped rolling hills screamed by. The road snaked around tight turns and through steep valleys where the cliff faces towered over her.

America pressed the green button.

"How can I be of service, Ms. Greene?" Brampson answered over an intercom.

"I seem to have lost track of where we are exactly. What is the E.T.A.?"

"About fifteen minutes, ma'am."

"Perfect. Thank you," she said and turned her gaze forward.

Anticipation fluttered in her belly. If this place was half as good as it looked to be online, she was certain she would be impressed. There was no use in focusing on the fact that she was to write a travel article, which she felt wholly unprepared to do well. America decided to enjoy the experience for what it was. The story would write itself. Or at least she hoped it would.

The SUV came through a valley and turned a sharp hairpin corner with caution. A wooden span bridge, like ones she had seen on Christmas cards, crossed a quiet stream. The bridge, on the other hand, creaked and shimmied under the weight of the vehicle. America held her breath, and the handle at the top of the door frame, as they inched across the structure.

Once safely on the other side, the road narrowed, and a village peeked from behind the next hill.

"Is that it?" she asked Brampson.

"It is, indeed," he said.

Coming around another turn, a wide flat plain stretched out towards the south, but fog shrouded the edges and made it nearly impossible to see the town from her position. *How am I supposed to get a first impression when I can't see the thing I'm supposed to be impressed by?* she wondered.

The vehicle bumped along the skinny road and splashed in a pothole. A sign that read Welcome to Christmas Cove hung between two pine poles on either side of the road, and her heart leaped with excitement as a cobblestone street materialized.

Victorian-style houses and flat façades lined the way. One by one, the buildings passed by the window. She couldn't help but notice the darkened windows and shuttered doors. She saw no twinkling lights strung on the evergreens, no garlands, no joyful tourists, no residents dashing out for their Christmas treasures.

"Brampson, are you certain we're in the right place?" America said. "This doesn't look right to me."

"This is Christmas Cove, ma'am." He paused. "Not what you expected?"

"No." Her response came out as a whisper, and she slumped into the seat back like a deflated balloon.

The main street passed by as quickly as it had appeared, and the vehicle turned down a gravel path towards the plain. America took the itinerary from her tote and looked for where she was staying the night. Knowing Mr. Janowitz's appetite for the finer things in life, she supposed the hotel would be where all the Christmas action had moved to.

In many older towns, resorts were brought in to revitalize the economies, and bring new life and jobs into an area. She suspected the same thing may be true here after witnessing an otherwise dead Main Street.

It was no secret that people preferred to vacation at new, all-inclusive resorts, where a well-paid and courteous staff would tend to one's every need. It only made sense, though a sad thought, that the old main street had dried up and been made irrelevant by modernity.

America eagerly watched out the window for a glimpse of her destination. Expecting to see all the Christmassy accoutrements around the next bend, she was confused when the vehicle came to an abrupt stop on the gravel road. Outside the other window, a lone cabin stood dark and vacant. A red painted barn in the distance was the first and only festive looking thing she had seen since arriving in Christmas Cove.

Brampson unlocked the doors and came around to her side. He held the door open and offered her his hand as she alighted from the cozy SUV. Her shoes slipped on the damp gravel, and she steadied herself against the driver's shoulder.

"Where are we?" she asked.

"This is where you're booked to stay for your trip."

"A cabin. In the middle of nowhere? Brampson, this is how horror movies begin. I've literally seen this before." She pointed to the small cabin and then to the fog rolling in and glowing orange through the dusky sky. "You are kidding me, right?"

America pulled out her phone and dialed Poppy. The phone icon flashed as it attempted to connect to a network. She tried again with no luck. "No signal. That's simply great," she said and stashed her phone in her tote. "Do you have service?"

Brampson shook his head as he lifted her bags from the back hatch and placed them on the ground beside America. "I'm afraid not." He checked his own timepiece. "The property owner should be here soon. He was supposed to meet us here, but it appears we've arrived first."

"Will you stay and wait with me until we find out what the story is?"

He nodded and shut the back hatch.

"I'm going to stretch my legs. Don't you leave me," she said and pointed two fingers at her eyes and then towards his.

After digging around in her suitcase for more practical shoes, she walked down the gravel drive. Grass spilled over the edges, and pine saplings dotted the ground along what looked to be an old split-rail fence. The gravel turned to wood planks, grayed from years of sun exposure, but with a kind of coziness, like a well-worn pair of jeans.

The terrain dipped down, and the wood planks turned into a raised walkway like a walking bridge. "Or a dock," America said and peered over the edge. Instead of a lake, there was only long grasses and small bushy weeds. No water.

The planks ended at a square platform where railings hemmed in a row of benches. A staircase went down to one side, and a flagpole stood straight in one corner, though there was no flag hoisted. The dock, it seemed, went to nowhere.

Behind her, a plank creaked, causing her to spin around. Through the fog, a man's silhouette emerged.

"You're not Brampson."

# CHAPTER 7

"The name's Leo," the man said. He held his hands up by his shoulders and opened them to her. "I'm here to let you in the cabin."

America's heart had jumped for a moment at the sight of the stranger. Her hand went to the center of her chest. "You gave me a fright," she said and put her hand out.

Leo's rough palm and sturdy grip left her reassured as they shook hands. His side-cocked smile and friendly amber eyes further put her at ease. America withdrew her hand and placed it on her fluttering stomach. The man was easy to look at.

"Your driver pointed me down here, and—"

"Oh, my gosh! Did he leave me here?" she said and marched past Leo.

"That is how car services work, you know. They bring you to your destination and then they . . . leave," he said.

"Yes. I know how it works. But I don't think this is the right place, and he shouldn't have left me," America said as her feet scuffed along the gravel path. "Isn't there a resort or something around here? This isn't the Christmas wonderland that I was expecting."

"Sorry to disappoint you. I don't know what you thought you were getting. I have a reservation for Ms. America Greene via Jet Trek Magazine," he said. "The driver said that was you."

"It is. I am her. I mean, I am she, America." She fumbled her words with each perturbed step. "Is there a phone or wifi in the cabin? I need to ring my office."

"Sometimes."

America paused. "Sometimes?"

"You know . . ."

"No, I don't know. I'm getting no signal on my cell." She held her phone out for him to see and wagged it back and forth. "I need a phone. Preferably one that works."

"Well, let's get you settled. I'll show you around the cabin, and then we'll figure out this signal mess. Okay?"

Though she was hesitant about a strange man showing her around a vacant cabin in the middle of nowhere, she had no real reason not to trust him, and no other options at the moment. With a grunt of agreement, she followed him up the path to the cabin where her bags sat on the bottom step. She palmed the handle of her roller case, and Leo's hand fell upon hers.

"I'll get this one," he said, and she removed her hand from beneath his. "You can grab the smaller bag. And your purse."

"Tote," she corrected him and immediately regretted having done so. "Sorry. I'm an editor. I have the unfortunate habit of correcting words. Grammar. Slang. You name it."

"Forgiven," Leo said and rocked his head side to side. "I'm used to it. My mom was a teacher."

"Was? Is she retired?" America said as she followed him to the broad front porch, painted white and black with a red front door. Looking out through the fog, she could barely make out the line of the dock at the bottom of the hill.

"Something like that," he said.

"So, Leo, you're the manager of this property?"

"That's correct," he said, and worked to untangle two sets of keys.

Parked on the driveway, his bright red pickup was quite possibly the most festive thing she had yet seen in town. It was only missing the obligatory Christmas tree tied to the roof and bushels of apples piled in crates in the bed, and it would have matched the Christmas card catalogue in her mind.

"Nice truck," she said and pointed with her thumb.

He looked around her and shrugged. "Thanks."

"You know it's missing some frost in the windows and maybe a tree tied to the roof, and then it would be perfect!"

"Listen, America?"

She nodded and waited for his response.

"If you're looking for Christmas, you've come to the wrong place."

Confusion washed over her. "The wrong place? It's literally in the name."

He pushed the door open and let her inside the cabin. The air smelled of cedar and time. She checked her watch. Even if she somehow got ahold of Poppy or the travel coordinator at the magazine, it was too late in the day to find other accommodations. Once the office opened the next morning, she could get in touch with someone and schedule a car service or train ticket out of there.

"This is Christmas Cove, is it not?" Indignation spilled from her tongue.

"Yeah," he said.

"Then forgive my ignorance, but where is all the Christmas? The pictures online and the brochure, the stories about this place . . ."

"It hasn't been like that for a really long time," Leo said. Sadness, or regret, pained his face. His eyes fell and his shoulders slumped as though her inquisition had wounded his pride in a way that she didn't understand.

"If there's no Christmas, then I don't see what my boss sent me here for," she admitted. "Seeing as it's getting late, I'll stay the night, but I'll be checking out tomorrow if I'm able to get someone back up this way to pick me up. I'm sorry for the inconvenience and I'll see to it you get the full payment for my booking."

Without acknowledging her, Leo rolled the suitcase into the bedroom and flipped on the light. Soft white linens and ivory drapes bathed the space in a cozy comfort. A fur blanket lay across the end of the bed, and an old touchtone phone sat on the far nightstand.

"Does it work?" she asked.

"It should," he said and walked around the bed. Picking up the handset, he held it to his ear. "There's a dial tone. No long-distance calls, though."

"Seriously?"

"Of course, I'm kidding. This isn't the stone ages. I only keep this thing in here because the cell towers are so spotty ever since . . . never mind," Leo said and walked out of the bedroom. "You can call anyone you like."

America followed him to the kitchen, where he flipped on more lights. "Ever since what?"

"I beg your pardon?"

"You said the cell signal is spotty since . . . what? Something good must have happened for the story to end on that note. I'm an editor, remember?"

"It wasn't something good, it was something bad," Leo

said and shifted subjects. "The fridge is stocked with some essentials, and the pantry, too."

"Thanks," America said and opened the fridge door. He had supplied everything she might need, from bread to eggs, a variety of wine, milk, and produce. A guilty pang hit her stomach that she was planning to depart the next day, and he had gone to such lengths ensuring she would have a pleasant stay at the cabin. She closed the door. "What was so bad?"

"It's in the past. Really. And there's nothing we, the city I mean, can do about it," he said with a sharp point. "The reality is that cell service is hit or miss, and there's a phone, albeit an antique one, that you can use. So, have at it."

America was sure there was more, way more, to his tale. No matter how long she played twenty-questions with the man, he didn't sound like he was in the mood to give up anything else.

While she had inspected the fridge contents, he had made his way to the door. "What time should I expect you out tomorrow?"

"Whenever the driver gets back, I suppose. Midday? Is that agreeable?" she asked.

With a nod, Leo opened the door, and a rush of cool, fresh air filled the space. "If you need anything, my number is on the fridge. Don't hesitate to ring me."

She wanted to say something. Anything. A thank you. An apology. Any variation of a salutation would have worked fine, but she was dumbstruck by his kind consideration of her predicament. She simply stood in her indecision to act and watched him pull the door nearly closed.

Through the crack, he said, "All righty then. Have a pleasant evening," and pulled the door tight.

# CHAPTER 8

LEO BEAT THE SIDE OF HIS BALLED-UP FIST ON EDWIN'S FRONT door, and a light flickered to life beside the window. He kicked the ground and scuffed his foot along the coir door-mat, where one would knock snow from their boots. But alas, there was no snow, just disappointment of a different kind in the air.

"What is going on out here?" Edwin said as he cracked open the door. "Oh, it's you. Come on in."

Leo headed straight for the kitchen. "You got a new brew?"

"On tap." Edwin said.

Leo didn't even care about the flavor, though he enjoyed taste-testing Edwin's craft beers whenever he created a new batch. On the wall above the butcher-block bar hung mugs and steins that Edwin had collected from his travels around the world. Leo took his favorite off the hook and tilted it under the tap. Pulling the lever, the amber liquid bubbled out and filled the stein. Like a professional bar-jack, he released the tap without overflowing the rim.

"You want to tell me what's going on?" Edwin said and took an etched gray mug down from the hook on the wall.

Not ready to answer, Leo sipped the chilled beer and savored the taste and crispness of apples and pumpkin. The fresh flavor surprised him, not because it hit the autumn nail on the head, but because Edwin's flavors usually leaned towards the practical and away from the enjoyable. This one was anything but standard. The man's improvements had not gone unnoticed.

"This is really good," Leo said and placed the drink on the counter.

"I tried something different."

"I can tell," Leo said and nodded his approval.

Edwin pulled Leo's mug across the counter and held it hostage. "You can have it back when you tell me what you're doing here."

"You know, I can just fill up another mug," Leo pointed at the rack of hooks filled with a dozen or more steins. Edwin's unamused face told him to get to it. "I met the woman—"

"Is she pretty?" Edwin interrupted.

"Does that matter?" Leo said and reached for his mug, but Edwin pulled it just out of Leo's reach.

"It might," Edwin teased.

"Fine. She was pretty, but I didn't really notice because she was too busy criticizing the lack of holiday décor. And not just at the cabin. Apparently, our town isn't festive enough for her liking."

"Our town, and the cabin for that matter, has absolutely no festive anything. Are you surprised? I told you we should have decorated the cabin earlier." Edwin pushed the mug back down the counter to Leo, satisfied with the answer Leo had offered.

"I know, and it pains me to admit that you may have been

right" Leo had a long drink. "She said she's checking out tomorrow."

The booking was the first one he'd received in a while, and even though she mentioned paying him for the whole booking, he wouldn't take the money. No matter how much he needed it, it felt a little like stealing. He would just hope for another booking in the new year. And perhaps he had stumbled upon a clientele he had previously been unaware of. Even during the summer months, writers would want somewhere quiet to come and work. Somewhere with breathtaking, albeit dry, scenery.

Leo snapped his fingers. "You know how we're always looking at ways to revitalize the area. What do you think about hosting retreats? Health and wellness folks could come in the spring or fall. Writers and such could come in the winter. Fitness types could come in summer. It could work."

"What made you think of that?" Edwin said and pulled up a stool to the counter for himself and one for Leo.

"She's a writer. And it got me thinking that other people may want to come stay here for some peace and quiet."

Edwin laughed. "Okay. But you said she's leaving. Not really a ringing endorsement."

"It was a thought. I just wish I had more answers," Leo said. "This place means so much to me, you know? I wanted to become mayor so I could make a difference here, but there's not much I can do when we can barely afford basic city functions."

"Don't beat yourself up about it. You only won by ten votes."

"I was the only person on the ballot." Leo downed the remainder of his beer and licked his lips, wanting another. "Carol got three votes, and she wasn't even running."

"Even if your idea could work, there's no money in the

town budget, or the resources to support an influx of people here," Edwin said and refilled Leo's stein.

"Thanks for this." Leo raised his mug to Edwin. "Cheers." The mugs crashed together, and beer spilled on the wood counter. "You know what would help? I need the woman to stay and write her article. It would be free advertising."

"And what happens when word gets out? Where will the people stay? Your cabin is the only respectable structure in town that can support guests. And how many can you fit in there? Six?"

"Five, actually."

Leo didn't mind Edwin's direct and somewhat wise line of thinking. And the truth of it was, no matter what Leo did, there would always be challenges. He needed to do something, or the town was doomed.

"You know what my father taught me when I would face something hard? He would say, 'Take the first right step and let tomorrow's problems worry about themselves,'" Leo said, and let a sip of beer cool his mind. "Getting her to stay is the first problem, and one I'm guessing won't be easy. But what if I get her to stay and write about the Cove? Some publicity might help this town get back on track."

Edwin downed the rest of his drink and walked around to the sink. While washing his mug, he stayed quiet. Leo could tell by the way the old man's eyes shifted back and forth that he was weighing things in his head. Edwin's vast life experience was something that Leo had come to lean upon often since moving to Christmas Cove, and he didn't take their special relationship lightly.

As counselor and friend, Edwin had stood beside Leo every step of the way as he navigated his role in the beleaguered town. He wasn't likely to mislead him now. So, he waited patiently for the man's thoughts. Luckily, Leo needn't wait long.

"What would make her stay?"

Leo already knew. "Christmas. She seemed put off by the fact that there wasn't any here. And who could blame her? All the stuff online shows this place like it used to be. A Christmas wonderland."

"This is Christmas Cove. I told you we should have put some decorations in the cabin, but you didn't listen," Edwin said and took Leo's mug to wash it. "Give her what she wants, but make her think it's her idea or it won't be genuine."

"Isn't that a little sneaky?"

"Think of yourself as a Secret Santa, giving her exactly the thing that she wants for Christmas. And who knows, maybe you'll enjoy having something to do."

"You always know how to walk that fine line between friend and enabler," Leo said. "I have an idea. A peace offering, if you will."

"You mean, bait?" Edwin laughed. "How can I help? Anything you need, I'm your man."

# CHAPTER 9

AMERICA HEARD A KNOCK AT THE DOOR AND SAT UP IN BED, removing her white satin sleeping mask. She scrambled for her watch and looked at the time. The day had well arrived, and the knocks continued.

"Drat!" she said. "I'm coming."

She pulled on her robe and flopped the messed covers up over the mattress, reminding herself to make it properly later.

"It's me, Leo," the voice sounded from the other side of the door, with a knuckle tap on the sidelight window.

Lucky for her, she had pulled the sheer drapes before settling into the most comfortable bed she ever had the chance to sleep in. It was no wonder she had fallen so fast and deep into a restful slumber.

The brass knob was cold to the touch, and she hesitated before unlocking the bolt. *What does he want*, she thought? Perhaps he was ready for her to get out of there.

She opened the door.

"Morning," he said with a bright smile.

"I'm sure you're ready to turn this place over," America said and rubbed sleep from her eyes. "I overslept."

"I see that," he said. "But that's not why I'm here."

"I was about to call my office and make my travel arrangements, but it'll take at least five hours for a driver to get up here," America said. "That's if they can even book a driver for me today."

"About that," he said with a mischievous grin. "I have something that may change your mind."

Curious what he could be up to, she opened the door a bit wider. His smirk and a playful glint in his eye had her cheeks burning. "What could you possibly—"

Leo stepped aside and revealed a narrow pine tree about six feet tall. "Ta-da," he said. "It bothered me that you were so disappointed last night, and I thought perhaps this would help it feel more like Christmas here for you."

The gesture amazed her. "No one has ever gotten me a Christmas tree before. I don't know what to say."

He motioned to bring it inside, and she allowed him to pass before overthinking the situation. Leo brought it to a corner in the living area near the stone fireplace and fluffed the branches. "This should rest for a while before we decorate it."

"We?" she said and shut the door to the cool morning air.

"Why not? I assume you didn't pack all your own decorations on the off chance you would have a bare tree in need of decking?" Leo didn't see her shake her head, and he continued, "Now, can you get dressed in something warm? I have somewhere I'd like to show you."

"I don't understand. You know I'm leaving today, right?" she said.

"We'll see," he said. "Eggs?"

America stopped at the bedroom door and thought she had misheard him.

"Over medium? Toast?" he added.

"With butter," she said and entered her room. It seemed someone else was planning her day for once, and she was too curious about this man to put a stop to it. But her controlling, organized brain was going to have a meltdown later, she was sure.

Out in the kitchen, a pan thundered against the iron stove top, and porcelain dishes clinked against the stone counter. While he busied himself with eggs, America rummaged through her suitcase and pulled out a pair of jeans and a white tank. In the bathroom, she threw on the clothes and pulled her hair up into a loose bun. Stray curls framed her face and helped to hide the indentations left behind by the trim of her sleeping mask where it had pressed against her cheek.

During college, when her late-night study sessions had made for unbearable mornings, she had perfected the five-minute-face. There was nothing a little bronzer and mascara couldn't do. Adding some crimson lip stain, she was ready for the day. She nodded at her reflection in the mirror. "Not bad."

Through the wall, she heard a muffled ding of the toaster. America reached for her socks and boots and held them in one hand. She searched the bedside table for her phone and lamented that, due to the mysterious something bad that Leo had alluded to the previous evening, it would do her no good while in Christmas Cove.

She opened the door and remembered her sweater. Stumbling back in, she grabbed the white cable-knit turtleneck and headed out again. She stood poised at the doorjamb. Leo stared at her from the kitchen. His smirk turned to a chuckle as he saw her recover from her near fall, and she followed suit with a little giggle of her own.

"Everything all right?" he said with a remnant of his amusement still in his throat.

"Yep!" she said and made her way to a barstool at the counter.

"It sounded like wrangling cats in there."

"More like squirrels," she muttered under her breath.

"What was that?"

"I said, what do you know about wrangling cats?" Her boots hit the counter, and she pulled on her socks as Leo buttered her toast and plated it. The eggs slid from the pan and landed on top of the toast. He placed a cut strawberry on the side of the plate and slid the whole thing across the marble to her. Her mouth watered.

"This looks delicious," she said. "Aren't you going to eat, too?"

"I ate hours ago," Leo said. "Plus, I'm trying to get us out of here quicker. So, I figured me making you breakfast while you got dressed would help move things along."

"Are we in a hurry?"

"Kind of. I want to beat the fog."

America had a mouthful and nodded as she chewed. Leo busied himself with cleaning the breakfast mess as she finished eating. He shot a smile at her between tasks, and she averted her gaze to the crumb littered plate.

"Thank you, even if your motivations are on the selfish side," America joked once she finished her last bite. "Wherever did you learn to make eggs and toast the right way?"

"Years of trial and error."

"Really? Self-taught, I can appreciate that in a man. You made them just the way I like it. Breakfast was absolutely delicious. Thank you."

"You're very welcome." Leo clapped his hands and rubbed them together. "Now, what else can I do?"

"You aren't kidding about this fog, are you?"

"Time's ticking," Leo said and tapped a finger on his bare wrist where a watch would sit if he wore one.

"I just need to make that phone call really quick."

"I don't need to turn this place over right away and you can make your call once we get back from this little errand."

"If you're sure."

He nodded, and something in his strong and calm body language made America want to know just what he was on about.

She tied her boot laces and pulled the sweater over her head, careful to not get her lip stain on the white knit. She stood and spun around, looking for where she had put her coat, and stopped when she got back to Leo. Standing by the door, he held her coat out to her.

"You look . . . good," Leo said. "I hope that's okay for me to say?"

Heat hit her cheeks, and she tucked a tendril behind one ear. "Thank you . . . for getting my coat. I always know where everything is when I'm at home, but here . . ."

"Organized much?" he said and helped her into the red puffer.

"I like things predictable," she said. "Do I need to bring anything?"

"Just you," he said and opened the door.

"You're not going to murder me or something? Are you?"

"Ouch!" he said and held his arm out for her to take. "Do you trust me?"

America had a dozen chances and a dozen reasons to turn him down, but like a tide being drawn into shore, she took his arm. "I do," she said.

# CHAPTER 10

AMERICA GRIPPED THE OVER-WINDOW HANDLE SO TIGHT THAT her knuckles turned white. Leo's truck bumped along a gravel track. No amount of cuteness could make up for the truck's fifty-year-old shocks.

"Relax. We're nearly there," Leo said and patted her knee with his right hand.

"Hands on the wheel," she said, and just in time.

The truck lost traction for a moment and they skidded sideways on the slick ground. Leo braked and pulled the truck to the side. Outside the window, America saw only bare trees and brown bushes. Their vibrant fall colors had long since fallen off. The sun, low in the sky, shone through the sticks and cast web-like shadows across the ground around them.

Leo got out of the truck, walked around and opened the door. He took her hand and helped her out. The ground was not only wet, but squishy from years of plant buildup mixing with the soil. It reminded her of the play surface at the park she used to go to as a child.

"Are you sure you aren't going to murder me?" she said

with a wink. His hand came around the small of her back and guided her away from the truck. "Where are we?"

Leo led her through the bushes to a small overlook, long forgotten by time. "You asked me last night about what happened to Christmas . . ."

"This is the something bad?" she asked.

He nodded, and she sensed the same sadness in him that she noticed the previous night.

"See that? To the left? That's the cabin you're staying in. And there, that's where we met on the dock."

From the new vantage point, America could see the grassy plain and a rocky shoreline. "This used to be a lake? The cove?" she said. "What happened here?"

Leo turned away from the scene and leaned his bum against a weathered railing. His eyes glassed, and he stared into the space over her shoulder. He took a moment before giving an answer.

"A few years ago," he began. "There was a terrible nor'easter storm."

"I remember. It knocked out the power in virtually the whole state for days."

"That's the one. But you see, the power went out because this reservoir fed the hydro plant downstream. The storm destroyed the dam, and the lake emptied out in just a matter of days," Leo explained, and she could see him biting back his emotions—and lower lip. "This place, Christmas Cove, was a destination all year round. In the summer, all these cabins were full of families on holiday. There were boats and skiers, dock parties, fireworks, you name it."

"And in the winter?" America looked at him.

"At first, after the lake drained, people still came for Christmas. After all, it is in the name, like you pointed out. But then, people moved away, sold their cabins, closed up shop, and soon there weren't enough people around to make the whole Christmas celebration worth the trouble of putting on."

"I had no idea," she admitted.

"How could you?" Leo forced a smile, though she could tell the reality had a nip to it.

"Why didn't they rebuild the dam and fill up the lake again?"

"Come on, America. You seem like a smart woman . . ."

"Cost?" she said.

"Follow the money, that's what they say." Leo kicked the gravel.

America felt a strange guilt in her heart that Leo must have noticed.

"What is it?" he asked.

She shook her head. "I just . . . I feel bad that I was so short last night about the state of things here. I had expected a Christmas town and got an old cabin in the woods instead."

"To be honest, I was in shock that a travel magazine wanted to do a story on my little slice of . . . heaven."

"You really love it here? Even without all the Christmas stuff?" America asked.

"There's more Christmas here than you think," he said.

"Why did the mayor want the magazine to feature Christmas Cove in the first place?" America asked as she processed Leo's story.

He turned his gaze from the view to her eyes. His head cocked slightly to one side, with one brow raised in the middle. "Me?" he asked, confusion contorting his features.

Just then, a semi-truck laid on the horn as it blew by them on the main road and stole Leo's attention. "My truck," he shouted and took off in the direction where they had parked. "Let's head back into town and I'll show you," he yelled back to her.

*Some Christmas town*, she thought. It was as bleak a setting as she had ever seen. There were no visible redeeming qualities, and yet, Leo loved something about it. A Rolodex of ideal travel locations flipped through her head. Not one compared in its solitude to the sight before her.

She whipped around at the sound of a mousy horn and saw Leo's red painted truck peeking through the twigs.

THE RIDE BACK DOWN THE HILL WAS BUMPIER THAN BEFORE when they had pushed to the top. The road wasn't any worse off, but boulders filled her mind. Leo, patient with his words, kept his eyes forward on the road. Although he grinned, America understood, or at least she felt, his sadness for his beloved town.

"I don't know how I'm supposed to write about Christmas Cove without any Christmas," she finally said. "Any ideas?"

Leo nodded, but remained quiet.

The truck turned a sharp corner around a grove of naked, gray trees, and light poured from above the incoming fog to illuminate a carved wooden sign at the edge of the asphalt. The sign featured two tall pines flanking the town's name.

"It's beautiful," America said. "But why is it hidden here and not on the main road?"

"That sign was commissioned over a hundred years ago when this"—Leo motioned out the window—"was the only road into town." He gazed at America, and she could see him in her periphery. "There's still a bit of Christmas here if you look hard enough."

All the while, America had been planning her exit from town when she should have been taking notes. Christmas Cove did have a story to tell, and she was the only person in any meaningful position to tell it.

In an unusual turn for her, America jumped into an idea before looking. "I have an idea," she said.

"Oh boy," Leo said with a nervous laugh. His hand combed through the side of his hair, and he raised an eyebrow. "Let's have it."

"The way I see it, the town could use some cheering up, and I have an article to write. We need to bring back Christmas to the Cove." America held back her excitement while she waited for his reaction to her suggestion. "Will you help me?"

Leo's answer came in the form of a smile as he put the truck into gear.

Back at the cabin, Leo got her door for her and walked her up to the porch. "I have some things to take care of, but I'll be back in the morning to pick you up. We have a lot of work to do."

# CHAPTER 11

Night came and went with another solid sleep. America looked at herself in the mirror, unable to believe what she had done, or what she had offered to do. Sure, she knew her reasons for wanting to bring back Christmas were purely in the interest of self-preservation. Wanting to succeed with her first article assignment was a huge driving factor, but the task at hand was so much bigger than anything she should have taken on. There was no denying her reign as the office elf, and she knew that if anyone had enough Christmas spirit to spread around, she did.

Now that the offer was out there, she would need to follow through. One way or another, she was getting her Christmas Cove experience, and an article drafted to prove it. Sure, she had enlisted Leo's help, but if she had any real chance of success, they would need reinforcements. America checked her watch. Leo would be back any minute to pick her up. In the meantime, she pulled her coat back on and tidied her hastily twisted bun atop her head.

The pine tree, so generously given to her that previous morning by Leo, stood in its bare state beside her. *There is nothing sadder than a Christmas tree with no lights. Except perhaps*, she thought, *one without ornaments too.*

"This simply will not do," America said aloud and rushed to the bedroom.

She flipped her suitcase onto the bed and unzipped the front pocket. Inside, she felt for the small cross ornament that she had stashed there before leaving her apartment. With the treasure in hand, she headed to the tree.

Finding a strong branch, she slid the gold string loop over the needles and gently let it out of her hand. The silver hammered cross glittered against the dark green needles and brown branches. America smiled, pleased with herself for the meager improvement.

"That's more like it."

In an instant, the cabin filled with Christmas cheer. Jingling bells seemed to emanate from the wood walls and into the air itself. Even the sound of clacking horse hooves trotting along an icy road filled her ears.

She giggled when she saw through the window, Leo drove a horse-drawn carriage down the road towards the cabin. The carriage bumped along the gravel and slowed to a stop in the drive. America threw open the door and ran out to greet the special guests. Her hands covered her giddy smile, and she shook her head in disbelief.

"What is all this?" she said as Leo dismounted from the rig.

"If we're bringing back Christmas, I thought this was a good way to start," he said and stroked the horse's mane. "Isn't he something?"

"I have to admit, I've never been this close to a real horse before. May I?" she asked.

Leo took America's hand in his. Her eyes shifted towards his waiting gaze and she felt her cheeks flush. She couldn't turn away fast enough. Under Leo's warm palm, he guided her hand and swept the horse's ebony silken strands from top to bottom.

"What do you think?" he said.

"It's magical," she said and stepped back from him. "What's his name?"

"Bingo."

"Is Bingo yours?"

"Not exactly," Leo said. "But we're good friends. Aren't we, boy?" Leo took the horse's face in the crook of his elbow and the two embraced.

"He's not a dog, you know," America couldn't hold in her giggle.

"Yes, but he doesn't know that."

Leo took the lead rope and tied the horse to a post at the end of the porch. From the carriage, he retrieved an apple crate with straw poking out between the slats.

"What's in there?" she asked, intrigued, and hoped that it was decorations for the tree.

"You'll see," Leo smirked. "Can we go inside for a moment?"

"Lead the way," she said, and he did.

Anticipation rose in her belly. For someone that loved the holiday as much as she did, each surprise brought with it the same feeling she experienced as a child on Christmas Eve. In that moment, when all the presents are set under the tree and only a few hours separate the gifter from the gifted, excitement swells with each passing minute.

"You look like you already got started," Leo said and jogged her attention.

"What?"

She followed the line of his pointer finger from where he stood at the kitchen counter to the corner of the living area where the tree was positioned. "Oh . . ."

"I think we can do better," he said.

"Are you disparaging my expert decking skills?"

"I would never," he said and took the lid off the box. "I brought you some lights and a few things I could find at the barn."

"Why are you doing all this?" she asked.

He ran his fingers through his hair. "It's been so long since this town has had something to root for. A friend of mine recently told me he felt like something big was about to happen here. Maybe this is it. Maybe this is what we all need."

Inside the box, a mess of mini lights tangled with a variety of wooden ornaments. Some looked painted and others had simple carvings on one side. America picked up the top one with a single finger through a string loop and spun it around. She placed the delicate ornament on the stone counter and traced the raised outline of a cardinal.

"This is very generous of you," she said. His thoughtfulness touched her. "You don't have to do all this. I'm sure you've got other things to take care of. A family, friends, a job?"

"No, no, and this *is* my job," he said so matter of fact that his quickness surprised her.

"You don't have friends? I find that hard to believe," she said and pulled out a few more ornaments. "I mean, I don't really know you, but from what I can see, you're very nice, and responsible, smart, handsome—"

"Is that so?"

America paused and her eyes made a giant sweep of the room before coming back to the center and meeting his. A smile pushed at her cheeks, and she sucked in her bottom lip, surprised that she'd let her mind speak for itself. "Let's untangle the lights, shall we?" America begged. "And what do you mean, this is your job? Because you have this rental cabin?"

"You could say I'm the welcoming committee for the town."

"So, you're doing all of this out of obligation?"

Leo paused and met her eyes with a subtle shake of his head. "No."

His one word said a thousand things and sent a thousand butterflies fluttering through her. She felt like a crushing teenager, and it scared her.

With the plug end in her hand, she worked opposite Leo and unknotted the strand of lights, finally meeting in the middle. Their hands touched, and she drew back. America took her end and plugged it into a kitchen outlet beside the refrigerator. The strand flickered on and off several times with a crackling sound that ultimately ended in the entire length burning out.

"There's nothing sadder than a tree without lights," Leo lamented.

"That's what I always say." America felt a tear, but not a sad one, behind her eyes. "Is there a store around here where I can get some new ones?"

"Does that mean you're staying?" Leo said while he wrapped the damaged lights around his elbow.

"Isn't it obvious? I already spoke to my editor. I brought him up to speed on the situation and he's on board with the changes."

Leo's smile said it all. He was pleased at the news. But his words spoke louder. "I'm glad you came here. And I'm happier still that you're going to stay. Is that too honest?"

"Not at all. I like honesty."

He gave a knowing look.

In America's mind, the temporary partnership with the man was shaping up nicely. With everything getting back on track, how hard could the rest of it be? She only had a limited amount of time to revive an entire town's Christmas and write an effective travel article about why others should put Christmas Cove on their destination list. She would be more overwhelmed if she wasn't so excited for the challenge.

"Well, Leo, partner . . ." She put her hand out and invited him to shake hers. "Are we in this together? Are we gonna bring back Christmas to the Cove?"

"America," he said and took her hand in a familiar way. "I'm all in."

They shook hands in an exaggerated up and down motion and giggled.

"Well, where do we start?"

Leo took the mini lights and chucked them back into the box. "Let's go for a ride and get some more lights. Ones that work."

"Sounds good to me."

Outside, Leo hopped into the carriage and reached down for America's hand. She was past the point of asking where they were going. And for once, she didn't care to control every moment of her day. This man sitting beside her, this stranger, calmed her every nerve with his gentle heart and sensitive patience.

She would have ruminated on the changes she felt taking place inside her if not for the distraction of the giant red barn looming in front of her. It was as though someone had plucked a photo directly from a page in a magazine and placed it among the rolling hills of swaying yellow grasses.

"Wow," she said and alighted from the carriage.

"Never seen a barn before, either?" Leo joked.

"Very funny. Of course, I've seen a barn," America said as she walked ahead. "But this one is positively perfect."

"Is that so? I hate to burst your bubble, but it's just a barn." Leo said as he worked at the padlocked door.

"Do you know why people paint their barns red?" she asked, but didn't wait for him to give an answer. "Hundreds of years ago, farmers would mix rust into the linseed oil used to seal the wood. The rust would redden over time, and thus, the red barn was born. Of course, this was useful for preventing fungus and rot, but they found the color helped absorb more warmth in the wintertime too."

"That's not exactly true," Leo said and threw open a large double door.

"Yes, it is. I'm always correct about factoids," America shot back. "I read it in an article in the Farmer's Almanac once."

"You read the almanac?" Leo laughed as he walked inside the barn.

"What is so funny?" she demanded.

"You're cute when you're stubborn," he said with no hint of judgment. "I was just teasing you about the barn thing. Your factoid, as you call it, is correct."

America nudged him with her shoulder and made a sound of satisfaction in her throat that echoed inside the space.

# CHAPTER 12

Inside the cavernous barn, America's pupils adjusted to the low light. Sun seeped through the cracks between planks of the outer walls and mingled with dust particles spun into a frenzy by her every step. Decades of use left the space smelling like the pages of a beloved old leather-bound book.

Leo left her side and moved off to one end of the barn. A slight curiosity told her to follow him, but a precarious stack of orchard crates piled high to her right stirred her prying eye more. She made for the crates, while somewhere behind her, Leo's feet scuffed against the dirty wood floor. The sound of metal grinding against metal caused her to turn to where Leo was throwing open the large double doors. At the far end, light flooded into the barn.

America coughed as she waved the kicked-up dust from in front of her eyes and yelled to Leo, "Hey, come over here and look at all this stuff." She clapped as the classic carol "Deck the Halls" played in her mind.

"You found it. Great," Leo said as he joined her. "That's the stuff we're looking for."

They wasted no time unloading the decorations.

Wreaths spilled out from their confines, and string lights with faceted bulbs seemed to glow in the sunlight, though no one had plugged them into a power source. Someone had taken great care when packing the ornaments after their last usage and had matched them to their color-coded painted boxes.

"What are we going to do with all this?" America said as she sorted items.

"You asked for Christmas. These are the town decorations. So, my question to you is, what are *you* going to do now?"

"I suppose this was my grand scheme." America stacked a red box, filled with assorted red ornaments on top of two others. Giddy beyond measure at the sight of so many wonderful Christmas decorations, a lightness filled her heart. "We're going to need help."

"Any minute," Leo said.

"You already called in reinforcements? But how did you —"

"Hello in there," a voice called from the driveway.

"Right on time," Leo said before calling out to the man, "In here, Edwin." Leo turned to America and spoke in a hushed tone. "Edwin is sort of a town legend. He'll get us anything we need. You name it."

Wasting no time, America shortened the distance between her and this enigmatic figure, so highly proclaimed as their savior of the moment, and put her hand out to greet the man. As she approached, his wrinkled eyes and thin smile told of a life well-lived, and his fully grayed coiffure was the brightest silver she had ever seen.

Edwin took her outstretched hand and pulled her in for a hug. She, feeling momentarily trapped with nowhere to go, patted the man on his back before pushing away. Leo, smirk and all, came to her rescue and put himself between them.

With a quick glance and a nod, she told him of her appreciation.

"Edwin," Leo said. "I'd like to introduce you to America Greene. She's staying in the cabin for a few days."

"So, you're the writer from the big city." He chuckled in a friendly way. She hoped. "Enjoying your time in Christmas Cove so far?"

"I only got in two nights ago. But so far, yes."

"Ha!" He laughed and walked past her towards the Christmas decorations. "I know you're fibbing. No one enjoys themselves here anymore."

"I can't tell if he's grumpy or funny," America whispered to Leo.

"No one can," Leo said and nudged her.

"What are the two of you planning to do with all this?" Edwin said as he rifled through a box of lights. "Wait. Wait. Don't tell me. You came for a Christmas soiree, and you won't leave until you get one."

"Not exactly," America started, and admitted to herself that the man was partly correct.

"Edwin, I asked you here to help us because I know you have nothing better to do today."

"I disagree with your assertion." Edwin rolled his head and turned towards the open double doors as though he meant to leave them to their own designs.

"And . . ." Leo caught up with the elder man and took him by his elbow. "And because out of all the people in town, you miss Christmas the most. The way it used to be."

Leo's statement must have hit Edwin in the softer side of his heart because when he turned back, he had a gleam in his worn eyes and wore the grin of a bested man.

"Please, Mr. Edwin," America pleaded. "Will you help us bring Christmas back to the Cove?"

"It's Pa. You can call me Pa," Edwin said. He made his way

back to the boxes of wreaths and ornaments and picked up a carved star with a black-and-white checkered bow tied to the string on top. "It's been a long time, hasn't it?"

"Too long," Leo said. "Will you help us?"

Edwin placed the star back on to the straw inside the box. "You two aren't gonna take no for an answer, are you?"

"Afraid not." Leo took America's hand. "This town needs this more than ever."

"And it might be our last chance . . ." Edwin added.

"Might be," Leo said, and America sensed there was something more, like when he had mentioned something bad happening with the dam.

Edwin stood straight and pulled his shoulders back as though he was preparing for a battle and saluted. "Yes, sir, Mr. Mayor. Corporal Edwin Kupa is at your service."

"At ease, soldier," Leo said and returned the man's salute.

"Mayor, huh?" America asked.

Leo shrugged.

America recalled the conversation she had had with her editor. He had mentioned that it was the mayor who had requested the magazine send someone to write a feature about Christmas Cove in the first place. It was all making sense now. How attentive Leo had been, how he had taken the time to show her why the cove had dried up, and why he was so enthusiastic about bringing Christmas back to Christmas Cove.

"I didn't think it was relevant," Leo said as though he sensed her questions. "Plus, it's basically a ceremonial position at this point. Not much to govern around here, if you know what I mean."

America couldn't argue with that.

"So, what are my marching orders?" Edwin said.

"You're up," Leo said to America.

Her hand went to her chest. "Me?"

"Yes, you. This is your brainchild."

America took stock of the items and closed her eyes. She flipped through the images she had stored in her mind from when Mr. Janowitz had pulled up the pictures on his computer a couple of days ago. The main street twinkled with thousands of mini lights glittering against the falling snow. Christmas trees dotted the storefronts, and wreaths hung from the streetlamps. She couldn't do anything about the snow, but she could help with the twinkle.

With a smile as broad as the excitement she felt growing inside her at getting to decorate a space larger than her modest walk up, she rubbed her hands together. "Lights," she said. "We should start with the lights."

With her small band of helpers, America continued sorting the crates and containers, handing the lights to Leo, who relayed them to Edwin. Edwin stacked the goods on a dolly and made quick work of transporting it all to his truck. From one of the bins, she pulled out a red Santa hat with white fur and a small silver bell sewn to the tip. She donned the headgear and Leo grimaced. "What? It's fitting, don't you think?"

"No. This isn't quite right," Leo said while Edwin lugged crates out the door and to his own parked truck. Leo dug through a box and pulled out a brass bell and red tinsel garland. He handed her the bell. "Now you can order us all around properly." He took the glittery garland and tied it around her waist like a belt.

"What's this for?" she asked. "I feel ridiculous."

"You look festive."

America could do nothing but laugh. "This is what I asked for, I suppose." She plucked a green tinsel garland from the same box and shimmied it in Leo's direction.

"Oh, no! I don't think so," he said and walked backwards out of her reach.

America sprang into action and chased after the vexing man. "All is fair—"

"In love and war?" he said as he darted behind an old tractor.

"I was going to say, in Christmas Cove." America used the tractor's red painted metal wheel rim to fling herself around. She would cut off his escape route and tie him up in tinsel. Her thought made her laugh, and she nearly missed him crouching behind a hay bale. "If I have to be festive, so do you."

Leo, seeing that she had cornered him, put his arms out. "I'll play along for now," he said and posed with his chin resting on his hands like a toddler beauty pageant winner.

She sniggered as she wrapped the garland around his neck like a scarf.

"Do you always get your way?" he asked.

"I don't know." America turned and walked towards the remaining crates. "If you mean that I don't give up on what I want, then yes. I'm not a quitter."

"I don't know much about you, America Greene, but I'm starting to get the impression that if anyone can do the impossible, it's you," Leo said and caught up to her.

"And don't you forget it," she said and leaned towards him.

The two paused and locked eyes. America knew full well that she was teasing him with her proximity, but she let her breath linger between them. His eyes began to close as though he was expecting a kiss to follow. *The poor fellow*, she thought and nudged his shoulder out of her way.

"Nice try," she said and picked up the next crate with more ease than she expected. It looked far heavier than it was, and the motion nearly flung her out of balance. Leo caught her by the waist and righted her for the second time.

America wondered if she should keep a tally for possible repayment in the future.

Leo ran his hands through his tousled hair, the way she had seen earlier. "I'll grab these last couple crates and meet you at the carriage."

# CHAPTER 13

AMERICA PLANTED HER FEET ON THE WOODEN FLOORBOARDS IN the open carriage and stood. "I can't believe I'm doing this," she mumbled.

"Whoa! What are you doing?" Leo said and fumbled the reins into one hand as he reached beside him to stabilize America at her waist again.

*Three times*, she thought.

"I have a plan," she said. "Can you keep this horse going straight?"

"I'll do my best," Leo said and took the reins again with both hands.

America took a deep breath as he drove the carriage beneath the Main Street sign, and she lifted the brass bell high above her head. In a rhythm that matched Bingo's trot, she rang the bell with more gusto than she ever had with anything else before. With each ding and dong, Christmas seemed to awaken a slumbering spirit within the town.

Her parade of lost toy soldiers, Leo, Edwin, and Bingo continued down Main Street. Edwin led the way in his faded blue Chevy truck. America and Leo followed behind in the carriage and she was glad that her clanging bell didn't spook the horse. Bingo seemed to pick up his pace with the sound.

To her left, a woman poked her head out of a second-story window, no doubt to investigate the racket. Lights flicked on in a shop window to her right, and another window lit up down the street a little way. By the time they reached the white brick building at the end of the road, there were no fewer than a dozen curious spectators standing on the curb along the Main Street route.

"They're either filled with Christmas joy, or they're irritated about the show and are currently plotting a citizen's arrest," America joked.

"Hold on to something," Leo said and pulled up on the reins.

America stumbled backwards and then forwards. She braced her hands against an ebony railing as they came to a stop. The final movement was all it took for her to lose all semblance of the balance and grace she had pretended to possess, and she fell back into Leo's lap.

This time, his hands wrapped around her midsection, and he held her tightly. *Four.* Everything inside her told her to move off of him, but the gravity she had felt since first meeting him held her in place, unmoving. America's arms fell around his shoulders in a far too familiar way, and neither of them attempted to part ways.

"Thanks," she said, "for catching me."

"It seems to be a trend," he spoke loud enough for only her to hear.

Edwin's car door slammed shut and broke their tension. America flinched away from Leo, and Edwin offered a hand to her. "Here, let me help you down from there," he said.

"Thank you, good sir," she said and curtsied once her feet touched solid ground.

"Will you look at that? We got their attention," Edwin said

and pointed down the street. "That is what you were going for with all that clatter?"

"Was it too much?" America said.

"We'll find out soon," Leo said and joined them at the bed of Edwin's truck. "Did you see that woman back there, the one who poked her head out the window?"

America turned and looked down at the darkened street. "Who is she?"

"Scrooge McCarol," Edwin about choked on his answer.

"Excuse me?" America said, sure she had misheard the older man through his mustache.

"Let's just say, if we don't get her blessing, then we might as well not even try," Leo said. "Pa, can you unload these crates? You can just leave them here. It's not like anyone's going to take them."

"You got it," Edwin said and had already moved three or four crates to the steps in front of the building.

"Is this the town hall?" America asked. "It's a beautiful building."

"It's town hall, the library, daycare, wedding venue, court-house, and community center."

"Seriously?"

Leo laughed at himself. "Might as well be. Anyway, that's why we're starting here. If there's one place in town that deserves to be decorated first, it's this place. I bet you can ask anyone in town, and they would each have a story of what this place has meant to them at one time or another."

America had no words, none at least that she thought did the moment any justice. Her first reaction was one of wonder and curiosity. Her second thought was of the camera and notebook she had neglected to bring along. The carriage ride and barn escapades threw her off of her real mission. She made a mental note to come back and take photos of Main Street before it was completely decked out.

She would need to turn the images in along with her article.

The photos of the town hall would be beautiful, she noted as she ascended the white stone steps washed in sunlight. A velvety smell of pine oil wafted in on the back of a cool breeze that followed them up to the doors. "I have one question."

"I doubt it," Leo said. "Only one?"

"I'm going to ignore that." America blinked at him. "I was wondering where all the snow is. In all the photos I looked at online, there was always snow."

"Hasn't been snow like that for years, not in time for Christmas anyway," Leo said and yelled down to Edwin. "Hey, Pa! When was the last time we had a white Christmas?"

"About the last time we had water in the cove, I imagine," Edwin's voice carried up the steps.

"Curious," America said. "Do you think it has something to do with the lake drying up?"

"It didn't dry up. They stole the water from us."

Leo's reaction had America on her heels. "You have some strong feelings about the matter, I sense."

"They could have rebuilt the dam here, but they didn't. And the only people suffering are the residents of Christmas Cove," he said. "Or what's left of us."

"I'm no meteorologist, but lake effect snow is a real thing. I wonder if there is something to it, even though the cove was a smaller body of water."

Leo shrugged, and America thought it best to let this one go for now. The subject was too touchy, and her prying would do nothing to help. She had no say in when or where a dam was or was not built. What she did have some say over was Main Street. She was there to experience a joyful holiday and help the town have something to celebrate. There was no good in rubbing salt in a clearly open wound.

Leo fumbled a keyring in his fingers and flipped through a dozen or so brass and silver keys.

She took his hand in hers and removed the key ring. "Which one do we need?"

Leo locked his eyes on hers. "The tarnished copper one."

America flipped the ring around and spotted the patinaed green hue. She pushed it into the keyhole of the enormous carved wood door and turned it. With a click and a creak, she turned the knob and pushed the door open.

Town Hall smelled only slightly better than the musty barn had earlier. It was as though the doors hadn't been thrown open for some time. Although, she suspected the smell was from neglect tinged in the sadness that the whole town exuded, and not from any true defect.

"What are we doing in here, anyway?" she asked. "I thought we were starting with stringing lights over the street."

Leo flipped a brass wall switch, and a wooden chandelier illuminated above them. The light bathed the hallway in a soft yellow glow. The colonial architecture's simple symmetry highlighted the space with comfort. Portraits and framed documents lined the walls above a shoulder-high chair rail, and several doors divided the walls into equal sections.

"In here," Leo said and turned into the second door to her right.

"Your office?"

"The mayor's office," he said and opened a narrow chest on the outer wall.

"Aren't you the mayor?" she asked.

"I told you, there's not much to govern around here," Leo said and moved a lever up.

"It sounds to me like you, Mr. Mayor, have given up,"

America said, and immediately regretted the accusation. "What I mean is—"

"You don't know what you're talking about," he shot back and slammed the wall panel.

"I'm sorry," she said. "You're absolutely correct. I don't know. But I see the way you care about this town and—"

"I'm really not talking about this. Can we drop it for now?"

"Of course." America nodded. The familiarity she felt with him was an illusion. They were barely more than strangers, and there she was, accusing him of lackadaisical governance with no evidence. The fact was clear, they didn't know each other in a way that allowed her to speak so frankly with him. Her goal was to help bring back Christmas to the Cove so that she would have something to write about.

Leo took America's hand and led her back down the hall and out to the sunny steps. She shied away from the sun as her eyes adjusted. A sound like bubbling soda fizzing in a can was all around them, and she couldn't account for such an unnerving noise.

"What is that?"

"Wait for it . . ." Leo said. "Wait for it."

Edwin looked over his shoulder from down below with a grin spread from ear to ear. His gay smile put her at ease. With a reaction such as Pa's, whatever they were waiting for couldn't be so bad.

A shriek came from beneath the street and traveled towards them like a metal snake tunneling through a granite cave. America covered her ears as water erupted in front of her and flew into the sky. She was certain she screamed at the unexpected sight, though she pretended the noise had come from someone else.

He chuckled and bit his cheek like he was trying to hide his amusement. Leo pointed back at the place where the geyser had been a moment earlier. A four-tiered fountain appeared once the spraying stopped, and the water that had been sprayed skyward froze and floated down like flurries around them.

Although her face was damp from the mist, she didn't care. The fountain was the first thing she had seen since coming to the Cove that seemed alive as it should have been. "It's beautiful," she said. "But why now?"

"We call it Hope Fountain," Leo said and moved down the steps. "People used to come here all year round and throw a coin in with a prayer for the future."

"Why hope and not wishes, then?"

"Someone once said that a prayer is not a wish, it's a vision of hope. So, that's what we call it."

"I like that," America said. "May I?"

"Go for it."

America closed her eyes and for the first time in a long time, she prayed. She prayed for her parents in Italy, that they were safe and happy. She prayed for the people whom she didn't know around the planet that needed comfort. And lastly, she prayed for the Cove. A prayer of hope and one of healing and joy.

When she opened her eyes, a profound calm washed over her. Instead of wanting to help, she now was determined to make it happen. She had experienced many great Christmases before, and she would have them again. But this one? It would be different. It wasn't for her. It was for them, the people of Christmas Cove. For Leo, the reluctant mayor. For Edwin, the soldier who needed purpose. The woman, Scrooge McCarol, down the street who she didn't even know. And everyone else who called the Cove home.

"Give me one of those wreaths," she said. "The biggest one."

Leo handed her one that was easily three feet across. She

ran it up the steps and looked for somewhere to hang the thing so that all could see it. An eagle with outstretched wings posed atop a round door knocker in the center of the door. She stood on tiptoe and hung the pine green wreath around the eagle.

When she stepped back, she saw how shabby the thing was. Its crinkled branches and crushed red bow had most definitely seen better days. She turned back to the men and put up a finger that said to give her a moment. Turning her attention back to the sorry-looking decoration, she fluffed the branches, straightening them and spreading out the wired strands. The bow needed a little less work once she realized that someone had carefully wrapped it up to prevent it from fraying.

America stood back and admired her work. *It's a start*, she thought.

Clapping echoed against the white brick exterior. Down the steps, surrounding the fountain, were Leo, Edwin, and a smattering of townsfolk. Smiles dotted their faces as they celebrated the return of Christmas to Main Street.

"What now?" Leo yelled up through the din.

"Wreaths," she cupped her hands around her mouth. "On all the light posts and doors."

Leo motioned for her to join him. "Time's ticking."

Time. She looked down at her watch. The timepiece, her most trusted companion most days, served no purpose here, she realized. There was no timeline for what she was doing. She undid the watch's strap, shoved it in her back pocket, and joined her new companions at the fountain.

# CHAPTER 14

LEO WATCHED AMERICA DESCEND THE STEPS, PAUSING SEVERAL times on the way down and looking over her shoulder at the wreath she had hung on Town Hall's front door. Joy lit her face, while curiosity grew inside him. He wanted to know where her love for Christmas stemmed from.

"What do you think?" she asked and tucked a stray hair behind her ear.

"It's beautiful. The wreath, it looks perfect," he said, though he was speaking more precisely about the woman standing before him, and not of the greenery hanging in plain view for all to see.

"This is starting to look better already," America said, and pointed at the crates of wreaths people had hauled down the street.

Although he hadn't asked anyone for help, other than Edwin, several people had come out to help with no prompting. Perhaps the town possessed more Christmas spirit than he had calculated. Christmas Cove hadn't held its annual public festivities for years, but people still celebrated in their own homes. Some people still put out lights and decorations in their yards, too. On the south-side road, the Townsends always wrapped their whole property fence line with white lights, and this year was no exception.

Seeing the people take up the mission made Leo feel that everything was going to work out. Edwin had mentioned that something big was coming. *Is this it*, he thought, *the something big?*

As he thought the word, a very pregnant Jenny Townsend waddled up the street. The baby had to be due any day now, and he was certain that Jenny's husband, Cam, had told him the due date, but he didn't remember.

"Excuse me for a moment," he said to America. "Keep working on all this and tell Edwin if you need help with anything."

"Sure," she said and flashed a quick smile before burying her head in a box of tangled lights.

Since America had proven herself capable and content, Leo jogged towards Jenny, who was one of the only people under thirty years old who still lived in town. She slowed her own speed as he approached and sat on a green painted bench outside the old bookstore. Leo joined her, glad for the break.

"I heard there was something happening this way. I had to see for myself," Jenny said as she caught her breath.

Leo didn't know what it was like to be pregnant, but it didn't take a mastermind to see that the entire process looked more miserable than was fair. *Sure, a cute little baby was the result of the cooking, but her oven looked close to over-heating*, he thought.

"How are you—"

"I'm fine," she interrupted. "Everyone asks me that. It's just a baby. I'm uncomfortable. All the time. And no matter what I do, this little guy isn't in a hurry to come out," Jenny said with short sentences, cut off with each heavy breath that she sucked in.

Leo took a second, out of concern for her, and scouted the street for any sign of Cam, but he didn't see him anywhere. "Where's Cam at?"

"General store." Jenny sipped on a bottle of water and found a snack cake in her tote. He wasn't going to make the mistake again of calling a bag with a strap on it a purse. He laughed.

"What's so funny?" she asked between bites and breaths.

"Nothing, I was just looking at your bag there and it reminded me of something," Leo said. "What's Cam up to these days, just waiting?"

"He's driving me bonkers. He asks me every three and a half minutes if I need anything or if my water has broken. I've been keeping him busy with little projects around the farm. That helps."

"He's getting more lights?"

"Ha. Ha. No. Well, maybe actually. I'm not sure about the lights. You never can have too many." She smiled. "He was getting some things for the bonfire."

"That's tonight?" Leo said.

Jenny shook her head while finishing another bite. "Tomorrow, I think. He looked at the weather and it seemed like the best night to do it before that cold front comes in next week. You gonna go?"

Leo looked back up the street, where a very enthusiastic America teetered on a ladder, hanging wreaths on light poles and fluffing every red bow in sight. Her white teeth glowed, even at the distance, and her laughter carried in the air to his ears. "I think I just might go this year."

Jenny made a teasing noise like that of a seventh grader and nudged her shoulder against his. "I didn't know you were sweet on anyone. Do tell."

"I'm not sweet, exactly." Leo said. "Charmed though."

Jenny stood and propped her tote back on her shoulder. "Whoever she is, you're a lucky guy."

"Isn't that backwards, the saying?" Leo ran his fingers through his hair, like he did when he was nervous.

"Nope," she said. "You thought I was going to say that whoever she is, she's a lucky girl. But anyone who knows you, knows that it's the other way around. Someone who can put up with you is a gem. Don't let such a trinket go."

He should have argued, but Jenny was right. He would be the lucky one. Leo locked onto America, surrounded by an ethereal haze, perhaps from the interplay of sun and fog, but the effect was the same. She had appeared in town like an angel sent from heaven.

Sensing his focus, she waved at him to join her near the fountain.

"It was nice to see you, Jenny. Tell Cam hello for me."

Jenny began across the street and paused. "Do you need his help with all this?"

"I'll let him know. Thanks." All the support and offers of help filled Leo with gratitude. He'd become mayor right before the storm and had never felt more like a real mayor than he did at that very moment. Mayors would always have some crisis or thing to fix, and as he approached the fountain, he was proven correct. "What happened?"

"Edwin thinks it's the breaker," America said. "You want to check it out?"

Leo took her by the hand and spun her towards the building. They would be checking it out together. He hurried up the steps, skipping every other one, and pushed into the grand hallway. Once in the mayor's office, he opened the electrical panel and checked each breaker.

"None of these tripped. It must be the main," he said and closed the box.

"Where's the main?"

"You're not going to like it," he said.

"And how would you know what I do or do not like?"

"I know you like Christmas, very much." He took her hand and led her down the hallway to a back staircase that led both up to the second floor and down to the cellar, off the main level. "It's now or never?"

America chuckled and pulled back on his hand. A worry line creased between her brows, and he wanted to massage it away with his thumb. "You're worried?"

"Remember when I asked you if you were going to murder me?"

"What is it with you and the murder stuff?" He thought quickly how he would explain away a murder and produced nothing. It just wasn't in him, which begged the question, why was it something on her mind?

"My assistant, Poppy, forced me to binge watch true crime shows last summer, and now I can't help it," America admitted, and her cheeks flushed. "I don't mean to offend you. You seem like a non-killer."

"How can you be certain?" Leo growled and felt ridiculous for having done so, but couldn't take back the noise. So, he pretended to clear his throat with a cough instead.

"I just know things." She winked, and it about undid him. "Let's get going."

Leo led the way, happy to be in front of her, and not stuck behind her where he would be forced to admire her mahogany brown curls twisted into a blob on top of her head. In front of him, a dim safety light illuminated the treads down to the basement. He had only been downstairs a handful of times. With virtually no town business to attend to, there was no need to be in the office, and thus, he had no reason to visit the downstairs level.

At the bottom landing, an old florescent rod flickered to

life. As it warmed from pink to bright white, the air lost its dampness. He knew it was an illusion, but something about a cold and dark basement had always left him feeling damp on the inside. Small, slivered windows sat just above ground level, and the afternoon sun spilled through the room, adding to the brightness. The lighter, the better.

"This way," he said and made for the stone wall near what was the front of the building. At the breaker box, he opened the door and saw that everything was in perfect working order. "Strange," he said. "What do you think it could be . . . America?" He turned around, thinking she was directly behind his shoulder, but she was gone. "America?" he said, and his voice echoed against the walls.

"I'm over here. Take a look at this stuff."

America had stumbled on to the shelves filled with archived photographs. "You're like a little mouse, always hunting for something good."

She ignored him and said, "Did you know all of this was down here? Some of these photos will be great for the article. If that's all right, I mean."

"As long as you bring them back, I don't see what it can hurt."

He watched as America thumbed through box after box and commented on the subjects of each image. She was in a universe to herself, and he had the privilege of simply observing her in it. Although he wasn't listening to her descriptions, he could tell that her heart was full of wonder from the way her smile grew wider with each box she dove into.

"You're so lucky to have all this history documented. Many places our writers go have lost so much of their past due to fires, storms, and theft. Please tell me all of this is backed up digitally." Her worry line had returned, only deeper with concern than it had been when she thought he was a murderer.

"I don't think so, actually."

"You know, most library systems will do the archiving. They all get federal and state funding for this kind of thing. You should look into it."

"I think I will. It would be a shame to lose all this. One of the longest serving mayors, nearly forty years, was a photographer, a hobbyist really, but that's why so many memories have been captured so beautifully."

Not sure what he would find, Leo peeked inside a box labeled with the year 1999. His heart began to pound against his ribs as he fingered through the prints. The colored photos, hardly faded by time, seemed to be peeled straight from his mind. One after another, he searched for a woman in a blue coat holding the hand of a little boy wearing a red puffer.

He gasped.

America stood at his side, looking over his shoulder. "What is it?"

With a shaking hand, he held the photo for her to see. "My mother."

"She's beautiful. And is that you?"

He nodded and put the photo back in the box from where it came. "In all my years here, I never thought to look at any of these prints. I didn't know that I was a star in the 1999 archive."

"Well, mister star, did you get the fountain working?" America asked and put away the last box she had gone through.

"No. It's the darnedest thing. All the electricity is on fine. Pa said to check the breaker . . ." Leo had a suspicion that he was being set up by the meddling old man who had not so subtly prodded him into spending more time with the big-city writer.

"That's what he said. Why? You think it's something else?"

"I do. Can you head back out on your own, and I'll join you in a few minutes?"

"Sure," she said, though he could see her curiosity tighten her upper cheeks. "Do you want me to come with you?"

Her offer melted away any annoyance he felt towards Edwin. "I got it. Thanks though."

Outside, around the back of the building, Leo spotted the problem. The red lever on the secondary power to the building had been turned off, and below the power box, the plug dangled from its socket. "Seriously!"

Edwin's cackle ricocheted off the brick exterior and right to the place where Leo had stored the melted annoyance. "Were you lurking in the shadows and waiting for me to come around?"

Leo's irritation crystalized as the old man slapped Leo on the back and gave no answer.

"You did this on purpose."

"Worked, too! Like a champ. You and the lady were inside for quite a while . . ." Edwin nudged Leo's ribs.

"We checked the breakers, and she got distracted by the archive photos. That's all. Nothing happened." Leo shoved away from the man. "Besides, America is very sweet, and I'm no murderer."

"Come again?"

"Nothing," Leo laughed. "Just something she said."

"She makes you happy. I haven't seen you light up like this . . . ever."

"Well." Leo walked with Edwin back around to the front of the building, all the while thinking about the cause of his happiness. Or better yet, what had been making him so unhappy that a few laughs and a smile were so surprising to those around him. "She's special," is what he landed on, and it was enough for now.

Waiting for him on the front steps of City Hall was his someone special. Beaming with delight and clapping her hands together, she ran to him, and he caught her in his arms. He swung her around and put her down. Her arm remained circled around his neck, and she planted a fast kiss on his cheek.

"You fixed it!" America applauded.

# CHAPTER 15

MAIN STREET WAS WELL ON ITS WAY TO BECOMING THE wonderland America had imagined. But while the others continued stringing the lights, Edwin gave her an important task. Though she knew she was up to the challenge in theory, she ambled with a degree of uncertainty to the end of Main Street furthest from Town Hall where, by all accounts, Scrooge McCarol would be waiting and, according to Edwin, would let her displeasure be known of the sprightly turn of events currently taking place along *her* street.

America steeled herself for the inevitable blowback she fully expected to encounter as she knocked on the lady's front door. No answer. Looking down the block, she spotted Leo and gave him a sharp shrug with her hands out. He motioned with a flick of his wrist for her to try again. If she hadn't been the one to ask for all this, she would have turned around that instant and bolted for the nearest highway. But, as it was, she had indeed asked for everything she was about to get. With the truth fueling her, she positioned her hand to knock once more, and the door flew open.

"What do you want?" the lady barked, and America understood why Edwin had called her Scrooge.

"Um, hi. My name is America—"

"I don't want whatever you're selling," she said and closed the door.

America promptly slid her foot in the crack and leaned in. "I'm not selling anything. Can I please have a moment of your time?"

"I don't read the Bible. I don't like strangers, and I don't want to talk."

"Please. Is it Miss McCarol? Edwin sent me to speak with you. He thought if we two could—"

America was cut off again, only this time the voice that spoke back had changed, softened a little. "Carol. My name is Carol. I don't know why that insufferable man insists on calling me Scrooge McAnything. He's one to talk! I haven't seen the geezer smile in years."

Carol opened the door and nodded to the side. America accepted the shaky invitation and followed her inside the darkened sitting room. She watched as Carol shuffled her feet across the threadbare oriental rug to the window, where she threw open the shutters. Light flooded in and bounced off the brocade golds and pale blues that defined the room.

"You can sit down, if you like," she said. "I've not had company in a while. And I've never met anyone named America before. Quite unusual."

What was unusual was how honest and free speaking the woman was. The kind of freedom that comes with age and temperament, America supposed, and wondered whether she would ever get to the point in life when self-censoring for others' sakes would rank lower on her priority list.

"I was named after my great-grandmother, America De Rosa. Her parents had hoped she would be the first of the family to immigrate to the States, but she never made it here," America explained. It felt odd to tell the story to a perfect stranger, but no one else ever asked. It was doubtful, in a place as small as Christmas Cove, that there were many exotic names to be found.

From her position on the worn jacquard sofa, America took stock of the framed photos scattered on every horizontal surface. Some were black and white, while others had the grainy look and washed out feel of a more serene time. "Your home is quite pretty."

"It's seen better times. Tea?" Carol asked.

"Thank you. Hot tea would be lovely," America said. "It's getting chilly out there."

Carol shuffled to the kitchen, and America was unsure whether or not she should follow, but Carol went right on speaking from the other room. "This house isn't the only thing that's seen better times. The town certainly has. My jawline too," she sniggered. "And this darn kettle. I can never get the thing to work when I want it to."

The distinct sound of metal being whacked with a wooden spoon rang in the air, and America rushed to Carol's aid. Upon entering through the swinging kitchen door, America became aware that the kettle was not the recipient, but the stove top itself was taking a spanking. "Can I help? It would be no trouble," she offered to prevent a murder.

Carol stepped aside. "It's the gas. I can't see the thing so well anymore."

America recalled a brief lesson her father had given her about pilot lights. She checked inside the cabinet for the valve and it glowed blue, just as it should. "This is right. Must be the stove." She checked the iron stove grate's placement, and then the flat disks that allowed for perfectly round flames, and spotted the problem. "The plate here is off kilter." America shifted it back into position with her middle finger, the only digit long enough to reach through the iron grate. "Here we are."

Carol stepped up to the stove, orange kettle in hand, and turned the knob. The flame clicked and sparked to life just as it should have, and America was immensely glad that she'd paid attention to her father's lessons.

"I appreciate your help, and seeing as how I now owe you one, why don't you tell me why Edwin sent you here."

America knew this was it, her one shot at gaining the woman's blessing for what they were trying to do. She hoped the small act of goodwill would stretch the chasm she was prepared to cross. Standing in her way was the fact that she knew nothing really about the town, and held no cards, and had no chips to play other than her cheerful personality. America knew Carol wasn't a fan of Edwin, though she sensed there was far more to their story, and Leo was still a wildcard.

"Tell me, Carol, how do you like the mayor?"

"An odd thing to begin with," Carol chuckled.

"Well, if I'm honest, if you don't care much for him, then I'll leave him out of the story. And if you do like him, then this will be much easier."

"Rest assured, I like the young man just fine," Carol said and took out two teacups with delicately painted blue and gold flowers and placed them on the kitchen table. "It's nice to see someone so young take such an interest in this place. Though, it may be too little too late. If you know what I mean."

"Because of the dam break? Yes, he told me," America sighed as she recalled his sadness when he had recounted the story. "Anyway. Mayor Leo and I want to bring some holiday cheer to the town, but I understand that you're a sort of gatekeeper around these parts, and I need your blessing."

"Is that a request, then?" Carol said, and the kettle screamed.

"Well, do we have your blessing to decorate the town and maybe get a tree for the Town Hall?" America asked as Carol grabbed the hot kettle from the stovetop.

"No." She poured the boiling water into the two cups and placed the kettle back on the stove.

America was slack jawed and at a complete loss for words. The woman had answered with such abruptness that it was possible she had misheard or misunderstood the request all together.

"Milk? Sugar?" Carol asked and plopped two white cubes into her own cup.

America waved her hand over the cup without an uttered word.

"I don't know why anyone would even care, even if you did deck every hall and string every light in town. There'd be no one here to enjoy it." She sipped her tea. "It's a waste of time."

"That's not true. You would be here. Leo and Edwin. Others and me, too." America couldn't help but feel the woman's pain at the loss the whole town had likely felt when the cove dried up. "I'm sorry about what happened here. But there are others in the area that would likely show up. I'm not asking for a lot. Just a sense of celebration and a reason to be thankful—"

"You're not going to take no for an answer, are you?" Carol asked. Her worn face scrunched in the middle, and the tiffany-style pendant light hanging above the table amplified her pale skin and hollowed eyes. "Why do you care anyhow?"

America chuckled. "I suppose I should have led with that bit. I work at a magazine. A travel magazine called Jet Trek. You may have heard of it." She waved her hands, realizing it didn't much matter to the old woman what magazine she was from. "Anyway, I'm on assignment to draft a story about Christmas Cove. So, you would imagine my surprise when I arrived here and found neither a cove nor anything remotely Christmassy."

"But why this place? No one has cared about this place in years. Almost everyone has moved out to better pastures and the rest are waiting around to die." Her hint of sarcasm shielded her genuine sorrow.

"That is quite possibly the most depressing thing I have ever heard in my entire life," America said and stood. "Listen, we would love to have your blessing, but it doesn't seem like you're interested in anything other than a pity party. Thank you for your hospitality, but I really must be going. There's much work to be done."

America turned to leave the kitchen.

"Fine," Carol said with a cough. "I just wanted to test your resolve, is all."

"Huh?" America was confused beyond normal measure.

"What, like I was just going to sit down and roll over for a city girl coming in here and wanting to change everything? Like a little pet project? No ma'am," Carol said and came alongside her.

"It is sort of a pet project, if I'm honest." America was a terrible liar and didn't want to start practicing now. "But Leo and Pa are taking it very seriously. And I'm sure there are others who would love to celebrate the holiday the way they used to. No matter what happens in the future, I don't think anyone would regret putting up some garland and ornaments again, even if there are only a few people here to enjoy it all."

"I appreciate your candor," Carol said and took America's hands in her own. "I think it's a quaint idea."

"You do? Really?"

Carol nodded. "And you can go tell Edwin that this

Scrooge has a heart after all. Then kick him in the knee for me."

"I'll do the former, not the latter," America laughed.

Carol led the way through the sitting room and to the door. "Is there any way I can help get this circus going?"

America had one question. "Do you know anyone with a big tree?"

"I'll see what I can do, dear." Carol winked.

# CHAPTER 16

OUTSIDE CAROL'S DOOR, AMERICA'S HEAD SNAPPED AROUND AT the sound of hooves clopping along the cobbled street. Leo waved like a loon from the front of the carriage. She waved back, then turned to Carol, who was standing just inside her home with the door cracked open. "Looks like my ride is here. Thanks for the tea."

Looking both ways before crossing, though she recognized that the learned behavior had virtually no purpose in the quiet town, there was still a giggle in her throat as she ran to Leo's side. A glimmer in his eye reflected the sunset. *Sunset*, she thought, *had the entire day already passed?*

"So, that went . . . well?" Leo asked and hoisted her into the carriage.

She nodded. "I don't know why Pa thinks she's a scrooge. She is lovely. Funny even."

"Funny, really? Carol? That doesn't seem right," Leo teased and pointed down the street towards Town Hall. "But did she give her approval for our little project?"

America's eyes lit up as she followed the line of his finger. Main Street looked nearly like the photos she had seen online. Wreaths hung from the light posts, lights stretched across the road from one side of the street to the other, and the mist from the fountain on the far side glittered in the setting sun. She was amazed that so much had been accomplished while she had been inside talking with Carol.

"It's magical," she said.

As she turned her attention back to Leo, he held two red cups in his hand and had a smile across his face. "Hot cocoa?" he asked.

"Marshmallows?"

"Whipped cream. Is that all right?"

America nodded back and forth as though she was considering the choice, all the while knowing that she preferred cream in her cocoa over marshmallows any day. Peppermint too, but she would go over that later. She had held out as long as she could before missing the comedic timing. "I'm just teasing you. I love whipped cream," she said as she removed the white plastic lid and slurped the sweet foam.

"You had me worried for a second." His eyes slanted to the side as she sipped the drink.

"Peppermint!"

"Did I guess correctly?"

*Did he ever!* Her arms flew around his shoulders, and she hugged him. This man, Leo, the mayor, kept surprising her. Not many people she knew could truly keep her on her toes.

She backed away. "Sorry. I got carried away."

"I didn't mind. I'm only glad I got your drink order right." Leo took the reins and ordered Bingo to giddyap. "Do you have plans tomorrow night, America?" Leo said, his voice shaking from what she perceived were nerves, though she had no clue as to why he would be nervous now.

Her instincts told her to say something smart. To deflect the question and ignore the flush in her cheeks, but she was intrigued. Leo was nothing like anyone she knew. Sure, he was handsome and funny. He was kind and patient. And, she admitted, willing to indulge her desire to bring back Christmas to his small town. There was something to be said about a man who would do all that and ask nothing from her in return.

But there was something more. The thought dawned on her that perhaps it was Leo who really wanted to bring back Christmas and it was she who had simply been the catalyst he needed to get things going. She was on assignment, but this town and its people were his life. If she just had more time with him, she could uncover his motives.

America's curiosity was too much to deny. "It turns out I'm free tomorrow night, and the night after, and the night after that," she chuckled. "Did that sound too eager? It's just that you know I don't have anything else to do. Although, I do need to do a write up and send it off to my boss. He knows what we're doing here, bringing back Christmas and all, but I'm sure he'll want more details."

It was Leo's turn to laugh. "Yes. I know what we're doing here. And I didn't want to assume that you had any more free time to spend with me. For all I know, you could very well have other things to do, like work, or talk with friends . . . or your boyfriend. I've occupied your day quite enough."

She caught his not-so-subtle question. "There's no boyfriend."

"Husband, then? I don't want to assume," he laughed again. Each time he did, America's cheeks burned and she had a funny flutter in her stomach.

"No husband, either. I'm all yours." America cursed in her head. That statement came out way more enthusiastic and available sounding than she had intended it to be. *What was he thinking?* Her head fell into her hands. "Just bring me back to the cabin where I can die in peace."

The horse trotted along the road that was now barely lit by the dusky sky. The fog had stayed to the south due to a steady north wind that brought a sharpness into the air. America shivered and wrapped her arms around her midsection.

"Are you going to stay silent all the way back?" Leo asked and shifted closer to her on the bench.

"I'm not risking saying something ridiculous again." Though she was wary of embarrassing herself, America leaned into his warmth. The daytime temperatures had felt pleasant, but neither were dressed for the rapidly falling mercury.

"Your honesty is very—"

"Annoying?" she finished.

"No," Leo said. She sensed the grin on his face but refused to look. "Refreshing. Endearing. I've never met anyone like you, America Greene."

This was too much, she decided. "Are you reading my mind or something?" She looked at him. Her suspicions about his grin's gauge were confirmed, and only widened with the pause that danced between them. "I've never met anyone like you, either."

Leo didn't say anything. It was as though they were each sizing the implications of the revelation. She desperately wanted to know what was traversing his mind. Hers, meanwhile, swam with all the silly dreaming of a young woman still in her youth. The version of herself that would doodle his name in her Trapper Keeper, the one that would pass notes to him in biology, and the one who would have begged to switch lockers with a friend just to be nearer to him.

What was happening to her? She had an assignment to do. And crushing on the small-town mayor of Nowheresville was not on the agenda. She looked at his face, with its strong jawline covered in two- or three-day-old stubble, his serious brows, and his red lips, and weighed the harm in enjoying the man's company.

"Did you say something?" Leo asked with a giggle in his throat that he attempted to disguise as a cough.

"Um . . . I don't think so." America scoured her memory. Had she said something aloud that she meant to keep to herself? "Did I say something about a Trapper Keeper or locker?"

Another laugh. "No. But now you have me fully engaged."

The way he strung out the word *engaged* made her think that was the word she had accidentally said aloud. It was better for her to ignore it than to address the slip. A sigh escaped her the moment the cabin came into view. And not a moment too soon. She was glad that the inelegant adventure could be over for the night.

"Thanks for the ride," she said. "Should I expect you sometime tomorrow morning?"

"Only if we get a tree for Main Street. I'll ring you in the morning if we locate one."

"Carol said she could help with that."

"I don't know how you did it. That woman is notoriously difficult," Leo said and stroked the horse's back. "In the meantime, you can get your writing done. I can't wait to read it."

"Don't be so sure," she mumbled, and he cocked his head to one side. "Never mind. Um, do you have my number?" she asked and slapped herself on the forehead. "This is your place. Of course, you have the number for the cabin."

Leo nodded while he pulled Bingo's reins in. "I've got to get this guy to bed. And you have a little tree to decorate."

"Oh, no!" she said and covered her mouth.

"What?" Leo looked over his shoulder as though he sensed danger. "What is it?"

"The lights! For my little tree. We forgot to grab some working ones while we were in town."

Leo smirked and pulled out a box of brand-new mini lights from behind his back. "Multi-colored. I hope that's all right."

It was more than all right. It was the kindest thing he had done in a line of kindnesses he had shown her. She felt compelled to express her appreciation and flung her arms around his neck. Her forwardness must have taken him by surprise. He sat like a statue, and a smile pulled up on her warming cheeks.

Leo's right arm came around her back and held her close with just enough pressure to feel reassuring, not forceful. Her father's voice filtered into her mind, saying, *If it's too good to be true, it probably is*, but America beat back the noise and let Leo go.

Taking the lights in one hand, she said, "These are perfect. Thank you."

"We'll talk in the morning." Leo helped her down and waited for her to get inside before she heard him call the horse back into motion.

Breathless, she pressed her back against the doorframe and listened to the jingle bells fade as the carriage crested over the far side of the hill. "Tomorrow," she said and headed to the kitchen. She placed the lights on the counter and made for the wineglasses. As she poured herself a glass of red wine, she inspected the modest tree across the room and made her plan of attack. Lights first, then she would fill the gaps with the ornaments that lay scattered across the counter.

Someone knocked on the door, and America approached with caution. She peered out the peephole in the center of the door and saw Leo, or his back rather. He stood facing away from the door, his hands running through his hair and kicking at invisible things on the front porch.

America covered her lips with her fingers and held in a giggle as she opened the door. He turned and was white as the ghost from Christmas past. She failed to hold in her giggle at the sight. Her eyes searched for answers.

"What are you doing here? I didn't hear you coming—"

"I wanted you to know," he interrupted. "I like you."

"I like you too." The words left her mouth before her mind had time to stop her. She really did like him. She stood there, waiting for him to say something else.

He stilled his fidgeting and approached her. His hand came around the small of her back and the other grazed against the back of her hand hanging at her side. He was going to kiss her. She was sure of it. There was part of her that wanted to kiss him too. She licked her lips and sucked in her bottom one as she felt her eyes widen with anticipation.

Leo must have noticed her flushed face, and he looked away, down to her hand. His fingers traced the shape of her arm up to her elbow and to her shoulder, where he paused again. His eyes shifted to hers. They stood there, wrapped in winter's breath, waiting for the other to make the next move.

She swallowed hard.

He blinked.

And the moment passed them by.

Releasing her, he stood back at a safe distance and brushed his hair back again. "See you tomorrow," he said and headed back to his truck.

There was no looking back, just an exit from an exhilarating encounter that she hoped would happen again someday. Once her breath was back to normal, she headed inside, like an elf on a mission, and determined to make the most of that bare tree.

# CHAPTER 17

LEO STARED AT THE TELEVISION. A BLIND-DATE SHOW, WHERE couples humiliated themselves with ridiculous tasks and competed against other pairs, was on. He had laughed during the segment when two teams went head-to-head gift-wrapping one another. Now the segment switched to a cooking challenge, and all Leo could think about was when he had prepared eggs and toast for America.

He switched off the television and looked around his home, a small fifth-wheel he had purchased as a temporary domicile while he built his forever house on the bank of the cove. The trailer was never meant to be permanent. Now, five years later, it was a daily reminder of where his dreams and reality had disconnected.

On the stove, a pile of folded laundry teetered on the brink of collapse, and the stack of Cup Noodles in the corner looked more at home in a dorm room than a mayor's house. Leo stood and walked to the counter, picked up his laundry, and took it to the bedroom where he put the things inside a built-in dresser. As he turned around, he saw the bed was completely unmade, and couldn't recall the last time he had done it up properly. His mother would have had a thing or two to say about it if she was there to see it.

Leo missed his mother at that moment, and made the bed in a way that she would have been proud of. After making the bed up, he turned his attention to the kitchen area, where the few dishes he owned sat dirty in the small sink. Leo ran the water and squirted some blue dish soap directly onto the mess, wishing he had a dishwasher. The tedious task was a welcome distraction from America's olive skin and black hair flashing in his mind.

As he put the last clean bowl in the one upper cabinet, he took stock of the space. Now clean, it was missing something, anything lively. Leo pictured a small decorated and lit Christmas tree sitting atop the table, and some string lights hung along the ceiling. He couldn't help but think how nice it would be for someone, perhaps a beautiful single writer, to bring him a tree.

Leo bit his lips at the thought of America again. He had done only a mediocre job at temporarily diverting his attention, but she was back in the forefront. His own face laughed back at him in the reflection of the dark exterior windows, and he saw a man in distress.

"How can I be so stupid?" he asked himself, and pulled the shades down. "This is never going to work!"

"What's not going to work?" Edwin called from outside the door.

Leo opened the door outwards and nearly took Edwin out. "Sorry, Pa. You can hear me from out there?"

"Those walls are as thin as cardboard," he said.

Leo motioned the man to enter. "Good to know. Now, what are you doing here? It's nearly midnight."

"Exactly," Edwin said.

Leo was missing something. "What exactly—?"

"I'm here, reporting for duty. Now, get your coat."

"It sounds like I'm the one needing to follow orders," Leo quipped and grabbed his coat from the dining bench. "Where are we going?"

"You'll see." Edwin smirked, which made Leo nervous. "If I tell you, I'm afraid you won't come."

"Oh, goodness gracious. Do I have a choice?"

"No. Now get in the truck."

Leo obeyed, mostly because Edwin never gave orders, and sleep seemed a million miles away. In all the years that Leo had been loitering in his trailer on Edwin's property, the old man had never once knocked on his door at midnight. Whatever was afoot, Leo was in.

Edwin drove the truck over his plowed field and to a dirt road on the edge of his land, where Leo was sure he saw flashlights sweeping along the tree line. Leo was too afraid to ask and assumed he was about to discover the orders Edwin proclaimed he was acting on. The truck's headlights flashed with every bump until Edwin switched them off.

"Are you crazy? Why are the lights off?" Leo shouted.

"Hush. I know what I'm doing," Edwin said. "I have the eyes of an adolescent raccoon."

Leo laughed. Unsure of a raccoon's visual acuity, he kept his thoughts to himself.

Edwin slammed the brakes and yanked the wheel hard to the left like he was in a street racing movie. When the truck came to a stop in a cloud of dust and the scent of burned rubber, Leo practically fell out of the door and planted his feet on solid ground.

"I stand by what I said about you being crazy."

"Relax, boy. I did worse than that in Desert Storm. Grab those gloves out of the back, will ya?"

With gloves in hand, Leo followed the flashlight into the woods and found Edwin standing with an ax in his. "Pa? What is going on?"

"I'll answer that!" a voice sounded from the far side of a tree.

"Carol? What are you doing out here at this hour?" Leo said.

"I was told the city is in need of a tree, and I found one," Carol said and patted the side of a twenty-foot pine.

"Oh, no!" Leo threw his hands up. "Not this tree. Not here."

"But it's perfect."

"And it's not on our land. This road over here is the line between Christmas Cove and Elizabethtown. No. We aren't stealing this tree. You're telling me there's not a single suitable tree in our own city limits?"

"Nope," Edwin said as the ax head chopped into the tree's trunk about hip high. "You got those gloves?"

"Pa, you know I can't be a part of this."

"Suit yourself, but I would have thought you'd enjoy it." He took another whack at it, and Carol clapped her hands together.

"You better pull the flatbed over here," she said. "If we position it just so, the tree will land right where we need it."

Leo grunted and knew he was losing this battle. "Fine. Don't let the thing fall yet or we'll never get it into the flatbed."

Leo jogged to the truck, where he hopped in and turned the key that Edwin left in the ignition. He took his time backing up the truck to meet the trailer and realized that the equipment didn't get there by itself. Edwin and Carol must have been at this scheme for some time before Edwin retrieved Leo to help.

He got out, hooked the ball to the socket, and slipped the chain pin through the hole. Back in the truck, he maneuvered the flatbed in reverse to the spot where the tree, and his accomplices, waited. Leo could see Edwin in the rearview mirror directing him to the best spot. Edwin banged on the tailgate when his positioning was exactly right.

Edwin opened the driver-side door and thrust the ax into Leo's hand. "You do it. It'll take your mind off the lady."

"What would you know about it?" Leo could have shot back more, but there was no point to it. Pa was correct. "Fine. You obviously know about it."

"I knew when I saw the lights on in your house that you weren't sleeping. And I know you normally have lights-out by ten. Ten-thirty at the latest."

"You watch me?"

"Not exactly. You parked your house beside my barn, and I can see it from my bedroom window."

Leo took a swing at the tree. "I've been living there for years and you're just now telling me this?"

"Never came up before," Edwin said with a shrug.

"I think it's sweet," Carol said. "Edwin's just keeping an eye on you."

Leo swung the axe again, and a chunk of wood flew out at the impact point. Out of the corner of his eye, he saw Edwin smile at Carol and then look away. "Something going on with you two?"

"Nothing new."

Leo recognized Edwin's dodge and took another strong wallop at the tree. The wood crackled and snapped. He knew one or two more chops at the front side would topple the tree. If he did it right, it would fall gently to the flatbed, and they could get out of there. Since it was late, and they were in the midst of committing a crime, he took two deep breaths.

Aiming, he took a practice swing to check his spot on the trunk. "Light. I need some better light over here."

Carol stood over his shoulder with the flashlight pointed at the tree. She was far too close and in the danger zone. For that matter, Leo was too close for comfort, but he knew he had a better chance at getting the job done. He took her by the shoulder and moved her back about fifteen feet but where she could still illuminate the side of the pine.

Another deep breath. Another practice swing. Leo lifted the ax and let its weight deliver a final blow to the trunk. "It's gonna go!" Leo jogged to Carol's side as the wood splintered and shuddered to the ends of its boughs.

# CHAPTER 18

"Hello?" America answered the phone, knowing that Leo was the one person who would be calling her there at the cabin.

"We got one," Leo said on the other end of the line with as much excitement as a kid on Christmas morning has.

"A tree?" she asked and nearly fell out of bed.

"Yes, a tree. What else would I be calling about? I need you to put on some warm clothes and meet me outside in five minutes. We have work to do."

"How do you know I'm not already dressed?" she asked.

He laughed at the question. "The phone is beside the bed, and you picked up at the first ring, so I assume you're still lying there." His breath caught.

She could imagine him looking away and heat burning his cheeks. Though this conversation was to the left of appropriate, she enjoyed provoking his sensibilities so. "I'll be outside in five."

Just as she had done the day before, America pulled on a pair of worn denim pants, a tank top, and a flannel button down. Her hair's natural curls had sprung to life during her sleep, and she decided to let them go. On a typical weekday, she would not allow her natural hair to see daylight, and would opt for a sleek pulled back ponytail or tamed, soft curls with one side tucked behind her ear. This day was different. She found herself not caring how perfect her appearance seemed to anyone else. She was comfortable to just be herself.

For once, there was no pressure on her to be a certain way or meet anyone else's expectations. The people of Christmas Cove had almost nothing to look forward to, as Carol had pointed out. Most of them were waiting around to die. *How bleak*, America thought. But she was there, and she was determined to help these people have something to be properly happy about.

Leo's truck rumbled down the drive and came to a stop in front of the porch. She half expected him to honk the horn, but of course, he didn't. He opened the door and got out. America decided to meet him outside like he had asked.

"Morning," he said.

America took his hand and pulled him towards the open door. It was only after she felt his fingers flex around hers that she noticed her heart pounding. "I want to show you something really quick." Leo followed without complaint. She stopped short just inside the door and released his hand so that she could point across the room to the small tree. It shone like a stained-glass disco ball. "Do you like it?"

Leo walked to the living area where the tree stood and inspected it. His head tilted from one side to the other, and his fingers brushed along the branches and tested their steadiness.

America giggled at his show. "What are you doing?"

"Checking your work," he said with his back still to her.

She played along. "And the verdict?"

He turned and flashed his devastatingly roguish smile at

her. "I'm impressed. You made the most of the few things I brought over, and I've never seen a Christmas tree that needed quite as much work as this sad little guy did. Seriously, America, it's great. But now we have quite a larger tree to get Christmas-ready."

There was no arguing with that. She grabbed her coat, and they headed out.

The short ride into town was a quiet one. She didn't know whether the silence was awkward, or whether he enjoyed the stillness in the frosty morning as much as she did. All around and as far as she could see, the countryside glistened with heavenly flocking. A flight of black and brown cowbirds moved like waves from field to field in search of a tasty breakfast. Soon, the frost would melt in the sun's glow and the tranquility of the moment would dissolve into the dull amber and gray of late autumn.

At Town Hall, the fountain splashed, and the wreaths that they had placed the day before took on a new light. The energy had shifted. Somehow, the small act of hanging the greenery had made a substantial difference.

"Do you feel that?" America asked as she got out of the truck.

Leo came around and held the door for her. A smile spread on his lips. His eyes had a kind of life in them that no longer looked forced as it had when she first met him. Yes, something had shifted with the energy in the town. Even now, she watched the shop owners and residents on Main Street opening their drapes, turning on the lights, kicking the front door open, and talking with one another.

How long had it been since this scene last played out? How many mornings had been left to rot in the sadness that the whole town undoubtedly felt following the storm that knocked out the dam?

"Here it comes!" The excitement in Leo's voice had a timbre of wonder.

The carriage turned the corner with Edwin tending the reins and a jolly smile painted across his face. Behind him, he towed a modern flatbed trailer. And the trailer held the fluffiest pine tree America had ever seen. As it approached, she could clearly see its branches were like feathered boas and dark green like Scarlett O'Hara's velvet gown.

America clapped her hands as Edwin passed them and came to a stop. "Where did you get it?"

"It was donated," Leo said.

America noted his vague response. "Lucky break." She would push him for more details later, but for now, they had a big job ahead of them. "We'd better get to work," she said. Her excitement and anticipation caused her voice to sound higher pitched than usual.

Within minutes, the hubbub surrounding their mission to deck out Main Street had reached the ears of some of the other able-bodied men in town. They gathered together and made quick work of attaching the stand to the freshly cut trunk. They erected the tree in place in the same small plaza where the fountain danced.

People spilled from the woodwork to see for themselves whether the rumors were true, that Christmas was making an appearance in the Cove once again. If they did nothing else, America could consider this a success already. Sometimes, all a thing needs is a spark. Something so small can ignite a new life—in this case, a hopeful energy—to a situation.

"Good day to decorate a tree," a voice came from behind America, and she spun around.

"Carol, I'm so glad to see you out today." And she was. Carol's presence there would put a legitimate stamp on the activity.

"I brought some things that I thought you could make use of." Carol handed over a well-used cardboard box, evidenced by a long list of crossed out items written on one side.

America set the box on the ground near the base of the tree and opened the four flaps. "Ornaments," she said. "Pretty ones. Are you sure we can use these?"

"Better out here where people can enjoy them than sitting around in a stuffy basement, don't you think?" Carol said.

"It's very kind of you."

America placed an arm around Carol's shoulders. The old woman, with all her saucy banter, reminded her of her own great-grandmother. She had enough stories of the old world to fill volumes. America supposed, deep down, that some of her independent spirit and zeal for family came to her through the bloodline. There was a strength that came with knowing one's history.

Leo was up on a ladder now, slinging the light strands around the top of the tree. She peered skyward. "How tall is this tree?" she yelled up to him. "Twenty feet?"

"Twenty-three, give or take," Leo called down, but didn't take his eyes off the task. "Hold the ladder, will you? I'm coming down."

With her hands firmly placed on the sides of the A-frame, she braced her weight against his movements as he descended the rungs. The old ladder creaked beneath him, and she found herself wincing with each of his steps. The whole thing rocked as he took the bottom rung and jumped down the rest of the way.

"Close one," she said and steadied him, though she didn't know why she was holding his arms so tightly. He was perfectly capable of standing on his own.

America backed away, and as she searched his gaze for some clue as to what was going through his mind, a strand of lights whipped around the tree and landed, wrapping around her shoulders.

"Incoming," Edwin yelled from somewhere on the other side of the tree.

"Thanks, Pa. We got it," Leo yelled back.

Fully amused, Leo unwrapped the lights from around America and tossed the strand back to Edwin on the other side. America had never seen a town in the midst of being decorated. It had always been as though she would go to sleep in autumn and wake to a magically decorated town the next day. The number of workers it would take to outfit the city was staggering to calculate. Though she had attended plenty of tree lighting ceremonies in the past, she was fairly certain that flinging strands of lights through the air was not the way it was typically done. She bit her lip, but a giggle escaped her mouth anyway.

"What's so funny?" Leo asked.

"Nothing really. I've just never seen anything like this before. Oh!" she remembered, "Carol has brought us a present. Come and take a look."

Carol had since disappeared, and America made a mental note to find her later and thank her again. She pointed to the box and let Leo take a look. His attention shifted between looking at her and inspecting the contents of the cardboard box.

"These are quite nice. Is she sure we can use them?"

"Yep. I asked her the same thing, and she said that they weren't doing anyone any good in her basement. Plus," America added, "we have all the colorful ones that we got from the barn. I have a feeling this is going to work out."

It took all day, and the sun was setting when the last of the red and gold ornaments were hung on the branches. They had placed Carol's special ones mostly in the front, where more people could see them. Each ornament looked like a tiny model of a home, a barn, a church, and all the other buildings representative of their small town. Each piece of the expertly painted village had a number and year signed on the bottom.

How fitting it was for this year's celebration for the town to be displayed in such a beautiful way! And what a shame it would be if no one came out to see it.

"We need to hand out flyers, and let everyone know that Christmas Cove is back," America said to Leo as they stood back and admired their work. Some of the people in town had come and helped for a while during the day. One lady brought pumpkin bread to share, and another delivered pots of much appreciated coffee.

"I'm sure by now that every single resident knows about this," Leo said and motioned up and down the street like an airline ground crew. "Things don't stay secret in a town this small for long."

"Then . . ." She thought about their options. "Then we hand out flyers in the nearby town. What is its name?"

"Elizabethtown. And I don't think it's a good idea." Leo walked in a circle around the tree, inspecting and fixing, fidgeting really, the ornaments and bulb placements.

"Why not? Don't you want people to come here? Wouldn't that help everyone get back on their feet?" America couldn't understand his hesitation.

"Let's just say, the mayor and I aren't pals," Leo said, and she was sure there was a juicy story behind the way he said the word *pals*, but she would add it to the list of layers she would push to uncover about him later.

"Then, I'll go alone. No one knows me there. After I've finished passing out flyers, I can do some research at the county library. Is that all right?"

"You're doing it again," he said. "Dreaming big and getting your way."

"I'll have you know that I work hard to get my way in life. It's a skill like any other."

"I have no doubt. And it sounds like a fine idea," Leo conceded.

"I think it's a good idea as well," Carol said, having reappeared beside them without them noticing.

"How long have you been standing there?" America asked.

"Long enough to see the way you two look into each other's eyes," she said and winked.

America bit back the smart remark that was swimming through her head. It was true, she had never truly looked into a person's eyes before, the way she did with Leo. With any other man she had dated, there was a pause after about a second of eye contact in which she, or he, would look away. The simple act of seeing someone and being seen by them was as foreign to her as anything. Why could she so easily allow him to see her true self, and why was she not embarrassed to let him look?

"Are we going to light this thing or what?" Edwin said from beside the tree. He held an extension cord in each of his hands and primed himself to plug them into each other. "Can I get a countdown?"

The sun had set behind the hills, and the afterglow of twilight was dissipating at a rapid pace. She searched for Leo, who had run off when Carol startled them from behind. "Where is he?" she mumbled. "He's going to miss this."

A few townsfolk trickled into the plaza, though wasn't sure where they'd come from. The tree must have called to them, or the new spark of energy had pulled them in with its gravity. Either way, she was glad to see so many curious and glad faces.

Edwin began the countdown from ten, and the gathered people picked up his numbers. By the time he reached seven, the thundering voices converged into one unified and amplified sound with each passing word.

"Three," America joined in. "Two. One!"

Edwin shoved the ends together, and the crowd held its breath.

Nothing happened.

Rumbles of confused complaints and queries as to what could have gone wrong rippled through the small crowd. Edwin unplugged the two ends and jammed them back together again. Still, no lights.

As Edwin traced the cords to the power source, America spotted Leo bounding up the steps to Town Hall. A moment or two later, the tree lit up like a firecracker, and the crowd was awed at the sight. She was certain it wasn't the prettiest tree the Cove had ever seen, but she could be sure it was the best they'd had in years! The frosty night and twinkling lights on the tree were the first real sign that Christmas had arrived. Just like the light that shone over Bethlehem and announced the good news, so did this tree in its own humble way.

Leo came out of the front doors, and she could just make out the white of his teeth. He walked back down the steps slowly as though hypnotized by the sight. The tree, the Christmas tree in Christmas Cove, was back.

Soft violin music seemed to carry on the chilled air. She turned and searched the street for the source of the pretty music. Festive trills filled the plaza from everywhere at once. And then she saw it. Edwin, Pa, was sitting on the edge of the fountain with a varnished violin tucked beneath his chin and a bow in his hand.

"Oh, Holy Night," Leo said from beside her and nearly scared her to death. The music, it seemed, had put her into a trance. "It's my favorite."

She met his eyes. "Mine too."

# CHAPTER 19

"ARE YOU STILL AVAILABLE TODAY? TONIGHT, I MEAN?" LEO asked with a half grin.

America simply nodded. There was no reason for her to play coy. She wanted to be wherever he was, and he wanted to be with her. "Where are we going?"

Leo, however, was playing some kind of game when he gave a shrug for an answer.

The recurring thought that this was all some giant setup that would end with her abduction or murder ran through her mind again. Although an unserious thing to think, she regretted all those true crime shows she had watched with Poppy over the summer.

Her phone buzzed in her back pocket, and she jumped as though a bee had stung her bottom. It had been days since she'd even thought about getting reception in town. Leo had mentioned that the cell signals were hit and miss. This must have been the moment when it hit.

With the phone in her hand, the screen lit up, and she waved it in the air for Leo to see. "I need to take this."

America took a few steps to the edge of the plaza where

the music was softer, and the air was decidedly colder. She took a seat on a stone wall and answered.

"Hello, Mr. Janowitz," she said.

"America, I understand that you've cleared up the mix-up from the other day, but I wanted to make sure everything was well," he said. It wasn't exactly a question and she let him go on without saying anything. "Have you got anything for me to look over yet? We only have a few days if we're going to get this into the Christmas edition."

"Yes, sir. I know, and I'm working on it. Although I was an idiot and forgot to bring my camera to town before we decorated Main Street. It was an oversight, but I have a ton of notes," she said, though her notes were mostly mental at this point. "My copy may not be what you were expecting to see."

"Oh?" he said. "How so?"

America wasn't sure how to explain the reality of the situation just yet. "Well . . . it's hard to describe. The town, Christmas Cove, isn't celebrating Christmas the way we had thought. The online brochure was missing quite a lot of truths about this place."

"And you have become aware of these . . . truths?" he said.

"I have. But none of it will make sense unless it's in the proper context."

"And you're getting that context, yes?" His tone was unwavering.

She nodded.

"America?" he prompted.

"Sorry, I forgot you couldn't see me. I'm so used to video chatting with people nowadays," she said and giggled briefly before remembering to sound professional. "I think this story is going to be of great interest to our readers, I just have more research to do."

"And some photos to take, it sounds like. I know you'll

come through on this," Mr. Janowitz said. His tone changed from business to that of a friend. "I know I threw you into this assignment on short notice. So, why don't you send me the notes that you do have, and I can take a look. Sound like a plan?"

"I'll send you what I have tomorrow. I'm going into the neighboring town and will have a better internet connection there," America said. "I was already planning a trip to the county library. I also found the town's archives, and there are about a million photos to choose from."

"That sounds great. I look forward to reading your notes."

"Merry—" The phone went dead. "Christmas," she finished and stared blankly at her phone screen.

The violin music stopped, and the few people who had gathered around the tree began to disperse. She scanned the remaining faces for Leo's. His back was turned. It was a view she had witnessed several times since their first meeting. He slid his fingers back through his wavy hair and turned around like he too was searching for something. Or someone.

A shiver ran through her from behind her ears, down her neck, and to her core, as their eyes met. She was certain the trembling was due to the cold and not to the piercing way he looked at her. She bathed her lungs with fresh cool air and felt her ears pull back like a cat on the prowl. She hated the way her body reacted, while still being hungry for more time with him.

"Is everything all right?" he asked when he was within a couple yards.

"It was my boss on the phone. I was surprised when it rang, actually."

"Uh oh. Are you in trouble?" Leo joked.

America chuckled, though he wasn't too off target. "Not yet. You see, this is sort of my first real writing assignment, and he was checking to see whether I'm up to the task or not."

"First assignment as a writer?" Leo said. "You mentioned that you're an editor, but I didn't realize that I was your first. I mean, this story is your first." It was his turn to hold his head in his palm.

America laughed with embarrassment oozing off her lips for him.

"We best get you something good to write about. Now, shall we go?" Leo said and took her gloved hand in his.

Back in the truck, America's feeling of anticipation increased. She didn't want to ask again where he was taking her, or what adventure she was about to go on. No other time in her life compared to this one. She had never released as much control over her schedule, nor given so little thought to each mundane decision during her day. Getting off the proverbial wheel could even be fun, she admitted to herself.

Christmas Cove was unpredictable. No, that was wrong. Leo was unpredictable. She had witnessed a change in him since their first encounter at the foggy dock. He had gone from cold and defeated, to hopeful with a side of good humor.

She was certain there was an interesting, if not entertaining, story behind his presence in Christmas Cove. The kind of story she needed for the magazine article. If she didn't push for it, she was hopeful that he would share the details with her in time. The tale was likely much more than just the Cove and its lack of holiday cheer. The mayor had wanted the magazine to cover the city for a reason, and she needed to find out exactly why.

The truck came to a stop in front of the cabin. "Home? This is where we're going tonight?" Disappointment saturated her words unintentionally. She hadn't acknowledged what her expectation was for their date. *A date. Is that what this is?* she wondered.

Leo got out and walked around to open her door. "Come on. Out you go," he said and walked to the truck's bed.

She began towards the cabin, but stopped when he cleared his throat. He carried a picnic basket in one hand and a stack of plaid blankets in the other. Now curious, a smile spread across her face, and she met him where he stood.

An eyebrow raised and the same half grin told her that he was up to something that she would likely enjoy. He thought himself sly, but she was beginning to see that his mysterious edge was simply a shyness, not unlike her own, that stemmed from a lack of practice at romance.

They walked down the gravel path towards the dock. The crisp air mingled with the thick warmth of burning cedar. She could smell the fire even before they crested the last rise in the terrain. Flames licked the night. Gold, and red embers flew high before cooling and gliding back down to earth like hundreds of tiny fairies.

Leo led the way down to the banks of the dried-up cove, past the dock to the place where the pilings were embedded in the ground. The tall grasses of summer had laid down for winter like a spongy carpet. He put down his cargo and took the top blanket. She helped him spread it near the fire, where its warmth carved a comforting dome into the darkness.

"How did you do all this?" She asked, then noticed a couple sitting on the far side of the bonfire.

"It's sort of a tradition. Well, it used to be," he admitted. "We used to do this every year. There was never an official day or time, but people would spontaneously gather at the shore a few days before Christmas." Leo opened the basket. "Here you go."

"What's this?" America inspected the paper and pencil in

her hands. "I mean obviously—but what do you want me to do with this?"

"We write down a fear and then throw it in the flames. Once it's burned up, the fear loses its power over you."

America considered this for a moment. If she needed a fear, she had plenty to choose from. A list ran through her head of all the things that scared her. How was she supposed to pick only one? A giggle escaped her throat, and she hoped the crackling of burning wood had masked it.

It didn't.

"You think it's ridiculous," Leo said. "Never mind."

He reached for the paper in her hand, and she snatched it back. "I think it's beautiful. I . . . I just don't know which to write down."

"Would it help if I told you one of mine?"

She nodded.

As he spoke, he pulled out a bottle of white wine and two glasses. "I'm afraid I'll never find a love as deep as my parents had."

She noticed he spoke in the past tense.

He handed her the two glasses and opened the bottle with a simple corkscrew, metal with a wooden handle. Another couple walked towards the fire edge and caught her eye in her peripheral vision, but she held her gaze on him.

"When my father passed away a couple of years ago, my mother's heart was so broken, she prayed every night that God would send an angel to take her to him. A few months later, an angel took her away. I like to think about them together, looking down from heaven, and guiding my path. I want that same kind of love."

"I'm so sorry, Leo." She placed a hand on his knee and felt a tear welling in her own eye.

"I miss them both, but I'm glad they're together again."

There was no hint of sadness in his voice. Only the gladness to have been part of their lives for a time. He seemed to be thankful, grateful that they had given him such an incredible example for him to follow.

"Shall we toast to that?" she said and raised her filled glass. "To a love so big, only angels can carry it."

He clinked his glass against hers and the resonant tone filtered through the air around them. "I couldn't have said it any better." They sipped their wine and sat in silence for a long moment. "Now, about that fear of yours," he said and switched her glass for the pencil.

America needed a moment to think. "Mine can't outdo yours."

"It's not really a competition."

"No," she admitted.

She wrote the thing that scared her the most at that moment. It was a toss-up. She scribbled words on the paper and folded it into a neat square before he could see it. Leo wrote down his and crumpled the paper into a tight ball.

Over his shoulder, the couple who had arrived first stood and tossed their papers into the flames. She watched the bright orange edges of the papers char and then float skyward once small enough. The woman threw her arms around the man's shoulders, and their lips locked together. America's stomach fluttered, and she shifted her eyes away from the couple's intimate moment.

"You ready?" Leo stood and helped her to her feet. They walked to the edge of the fire where a circle of stones marked its boundary, though the heat radiated out from the center as a warning of where to stop.

America closed her eyes and then immediately opened them again. "Am I doing this right?"

He nodded and closed his eyes.

She followed suit.

"On the count of three," he said and began, "One . . ."

"Two," she said.

"Three."

The paper left her hand as though she was throwing a baseball in a World Series game. She wanted to be certain the fire would devour her fear.

"Open your eyes," Leo whispered into her ear.

The tiny hairs perked up and tickled her neck, causing her hand to reach up and cover them. He stood close. Too close. She swallowed hard at the sight of his rapid breaths condensing and dissipating into the chilly night air. Was he going to kiss her? Because she wanted to kiss him.

The tension was as thick as fruitcake, and just as delicious. Her mouth watered, and she licked the cold from her lips.

"Are you hungry?" he asked.

"Uh huh," America nodded.

"I brought s'mores."

"Some more . . ." she mumbled.

"No," he laughed and broke her trance. "You know, s'mores. To eat."

She shook her head and got her bearings. At some point, the two other couples had turned into three. The bonfire was hot and close. She stepped back to the blanket, where Leo sat cross-legged and dug around in the basket. Her lip licking must have made him think she was hungry. America placed a hand on her belly. It had been hours since she'd eaten anything, and her stomach rumbled as though on cue.

Leo handed her a poker with a large marshmallow positioned at the end of the tines. She held the puffed sugar to the flames. A new fear that she hadn't considered moments earlier crossed her mind. He was like honey. She was a fly. And she feared sticking to him and never being able to get away. The thought kept her eyes trained on the toasting marshmallow and away from him.

She preferred her marshmallow perfectly golden and evenly heated. Leo apparently preferred his on fire. His whole mallow was up in flames. He turned it over and brought it to her face. "Blow," he said.

She did as he requested with a stifled giggle. The whole scene smacked of harmless impropriety.

"Let me help." America handed her rotisseried marshmallow to him and got two graham crackers and the chocolate ready. She used the two crackers and slid his charred marshmallow off. Then her own.

"I didn't know I was sitting beside greatness," he said and dropped the pokers on the edge of the fire.

"I don't know what you mean," she batted her eyes. "Fine. I went to a camp every summer until I was about fourteen. We ate a lot of s'mores, and I got really good at building them."

He laughed through his nose as he ate his treat.

"And what's your story? No one ever showed you how to not burn the sugar?" she joked.

"I like it like this, thank you very much."

"Sorry," she said through sticky lips and a mouthful. Very unladylike. "So, Mr. Mayor, tell me. How did you end up here?"

"That's easy. I grew up coming here in summers, with my parents. You know, it's funny. We never really came in the winter, for Christmas, I mean."

"No?" she prodded.

"Once, or maybe twice." His face muscles eased into a pleasant, wide-eyed grin. He was remembering something happy. "I did come up here during high school once. My girlfriend at the time and her family were supposed to meet me and my parents up here, but they never showed up. Later, she blamed it on a snowstorm or icy roads, but she just knew I wasn't the one for her and didn't want to break things off at Christmas."

His eyes looked up and away as though another memory came to mind, and his expression shifted. His brows knitted together and formed a little u-shape crevasse above his nose.

"What is it?" America asked.

He was quiet for a long moment, his breath slowed, and his eyes shut. "The year when my father passed away, we had planned to come here for Christmas, but he passed away before our trip. Mom died in the new year."

"How did he die?"

"Heart attack. No one saw it coming." Leo shook his head and flicked a tear from the corner of his eye, though he tried unconvincingly to disguise it as a scratch on his cheek.

"I don't know how you must feel." She didn't lie. Her parents were happy and alive, having the time of their lives in Italy, while his were reunited in heaven. The thought was a small condolence to his grief and her guilt. "So, is that why you moved here?"

"I can't imagine anywhere else I'd rather be. My happiest memories are from this place," he admitted. "I only wish things were the same as before."

"Before the storm?"

"I moved here and bam! No cove. And soon after, no Christmas either."

She could feel his anger rise. She held his hand. "There was no way for you to know."

He picked some grass and threw it into the flames. "I know. It's just so sad, you know?"

"I can see that." America paused. "But look around. Look what we've done in just a few days. Perhaps this isn't the end of Christmas at the Cove. It can't be."

"Can't it though?" He took both of her hands in his and pressed them to his chest. "All I have . . . all we have is in here.

In our hearts. This place included. It'll be in people's hearts and memories for what? Another generation? Anyone who knows this place and how special it was will all be gone before too long—"

"We won't let that happen. I promise," America said.

"You can't do that, America. In a couple of days, you'll leave this place and never look back. To you, this is just an assignment, but this is my life." Leo began to throw things back into the basket.

America was at a complete loss for words. Was he correct? Would she leave in a few days and be done with this place? How could she know for sure, and how could she promise anything to him? He was, like he rightly pointed out, just an assignment.

Without warning, he got up. "I had a great night tonight, but it's time for me to go. I'll see you tomorrow and take you to Elizabethtown. Is ten o'clock a suitable time?" he said.

# CHAPTER 20

WITH A STACK OF FRESHLY PRINTED AND STILL WARM FLIERS IN her lap, America shifted her weight away from Edwin sitting on the driver's side of the truck bench.

"Pa, thanks for taking me into Elizabethtown on such short notice," America said.

He had offered to take her into town when Leo couldn't make it to pick her up. Leo's excuse had been something about a sore throat, but she suspected the truth had more to do with their conversation at the bonfire. He probably needed some time to think after she upset what would have otherwise been a perfect date.

She admitted that she could use some time alone with her own thoughts, too. Going to Elizabethtown seemed like the perfect diversion from her unexpected infatuation with the very handsome, very eligible young mayor. In the meantime, Edwin offered to help hand out the fliers while attending to some other business in town. America planned to pass out the fliers on her way to the library.

"And thanks for driving me down Main Street so that I could snap some photos of all the work we did. I'm really grateful to have met you this week," America said as the gray scenery screamed by outside her window.

"Can I ask you something, city girl?" Edwin said.

"What's that?"

"Why do you care so much?" he asked and cleared his throat. "About helping my little town, I mean?"

"For starters, I love Christmas. It's my favorite time of year," she began. "It's not the presents, or the dinner parties for me. It's a holiday where people come together. Everyone is a little more kind, a bit more generous with their time, and everything glitters. The snow, the ornaments, the twinkly lights, they all scream the Good News." A smile pushed her cheeks up. She could speak about this particular topic for as long as someone was willing to listen.

Edwin made a noise in his throat that indicated he was listening but hadn't yet heard a clear answer to his question. "That's a very political answer. I know there's more."

"You are correct, and far too wise for your own good," she said. "To be honest, I always spend Christmas with my parents, but this year they jetted off to Italy for a once-in-a-lifetime trip to trace my mother's heritage. And... let's just say, when I came here, to the Cove, I was expecting a wholly dissimilar experience to the one I was dumped into." America shifted her position on the truck bench and looked at the side of Edwin's face. "I'd never seen such a sad place. Everything here was dull and lifeless. No offense."

"None taken," he smirked. "Though, Carol might think differently. Everything offends her these days."

"You know? She told me to kick you for calling her Scrooge?"

"That sounds right. But she probably didn't tell you why I call her that." His brow over his right eye lifted with his cheek.

"Do tell," she said, glad to be talking about something other than herself.

"I was sweet on Carol. Oh, decades ago when we were in high school. She was on the dance team, and she was magnificent. I joined the basketball team just to see her dance at half time. We never spoke, not more than a *hello* or *good game,* until it was time for the winter formal."

"Let me guess," America snuck her words in between his breaths. "You asked her to the dance, and she said no?"

"Actually, she said yes," he laughed as though he was still in shock after all these years. "I was just as surprised as everyone else. Carol never went steady with anyone in high school."

"Then what happened?"

"You know, the normal, wholesome stuff. We danced the whole night, drank punch, and got to know each other. Oh, we laughed and laughed." He chuckled at the memory. "At the end of the night, we stood outside the gym doors. The night was cold, and she had a white fur stole wrapped around her shoulders. It began to snow, and she looked up at the tiny flakes falling on her lashes. Then, she dropped the fur and walked out into the flurries. That's when she slipped, and I caught her. I'm very chivalrous you know."

"I have no doubt," America smiled.

"She looked into my eyes, and I into hers. I wanted badly to kiss her, and I think she would have kissed me too, but just as I could feel the heat from her lips, her father drove up to the building, honking the horn. She kicked me in the shin and told me to let her go, as though I was violating her in some way. And that was that."

America's laugh bounced around the space. "That explains why she told me to kick you. And you've called her Scrooge ever since?"

"That's right!"

"It seems like maybe there was more going on. Like she didn't want to get in trouble with her father or something."

"Either way, I never asked, and she never talked to me about it. Like I said, that was that."

America laughed in disbelief. How easily a small thing can have ripple effects for years and years! Is that what she was doing, creating a ripple in Christmas Cove? Could she have a positive impact on this special place for the next generation? She thumbed the edges of the stack of fliers in her lap. Leo or not, her mission was clear.

"Uh-hem. You still didn't answer my question, and I answered yours," Edwin rightly pointed out.

"I was hoping I was off the hook."

"You're not. So, spill it."

"When I saw how sad Leo was about the town no longer having a Christmas celebration, the way it used to, I knew I had enough holiday cheer, and enough free time, to help. But I would only help if that's what the people here wanted," she said. "And by the looks of things, all the people at the tree lighting, the bonfire, and the shops opening their dusty doors again, I think people are craving the feeling of joy now more than ever."

"You're not wrong there," Edwin said and looked at her with a wink. "You breezed into town a few days ago with a kind of energy and light that we haven't seen around these parts in an awfully long time. I'm thankful for you, dear."

"Thanks, Pa. I only hope Leo feels that way, too."

"What happened between you two, anyhow? I know that boy doesn't have a sore throat. Worst fibber I've ever seen," Edwin said.

"I'm not sure. I'll need to speak with him later. I really like him, you know," she admitted aloud for the first time. "I think he's afraid that I'm using him for a story and that once

I get what I need, I'll leave and never think about him or this place again."

"Is he very wrong?" Edwin asked.

America declined to answer. Because the reality was that she would leave soon.

"You can let me out here," she said as the truck turned the corner onto Main Street.

"You know where you're goin'?"

"I think so. I'll meet you at the library in a couple of hours?"

"See you there." Edwin pulled over, and she got out.

# CHAPTER 21

THE WAITING AREA AT THE COUNTY MUNICIPAL BUILDING couldn't have been less appealing, like cold oatmeal. Leo's eyes bounced from the beige linoleum flooring to the cream walls, and to the matching help desk positioned at one side. The cold surfaces did nothing to ease his nerves about waiting to see the county lawyer.

Leo checked the white clock on the wall and watched the seconds tick by. He hadn't scheduled a meeting, and decided to stay and wait for a possible opening. There was a time when the dam had first blown out when he learned the importance of asking for things in person.

Leo had sat in the Land Commissioner's office, day after day, waiting for an answer about the new property lines since the lake dried up. And by golly, the man got him an answer as fast as he could, just to get Leo out of there.

Even being at the lawyer's office in person, Leo wasn't sure the lawyer would have time to see him at all, but he was willing to wait outside her door for the chance. It's much more difficult to say no to someone's face, and he planned to stay all day if he had to.

A pang of guilt twisted his stomach. When he got back to his home after leaving America at the bonfire, Leo received an email that felt like a knife in his gut. His plans for the day had changed in that instant. Until he knew more about the situation, he faked an illness and called Edwin for help.

America needed to go to the library and pass out her fliers in Elizabethtown, and Edwin was already planning a trip in that direction. Leo canceled their plans for no real reason, in order to spend his day waiting. He owed her far more than just an explanation about the morning's events, but also an apology for how he acted after their almost kiss. He was a fool and scared by the feelings he had for her. There would be time for penance later, but first, he had a different challenge to face.

Opening the email message on his phone, he read the signature line again: Janice Masters, Esq. The name matched the nameplate on the wall beside the door. He was definitely in the correct place. The only question was, would she see him or not?

The office door opened, and he stood, hoping to be called in next. Two women came out, jackets in hand, a briefcase with one, and a stack of yellow folders with the other. Because of their gleeful smiles, they must have had a pleasant encounter with the lawyer. A good sign.

Once the doorway had cleared, Leo poked his head around the corner and looked inside the office, but there was no one there. *Strange*, he thought, and went in. Two women had apparently just left a good meeting and there was no other door for the lawyer to have disappeared through.

Janice Masters's office was nothing like the utilitarian waiting room space. Rich, dark wood bookshelves, spilling with volumes of law books, encyclopedias, and various nonfiction, lined the far wall. A large desk rivaling the one in the Oval Office sat dead center, and rich, red velvet curtains framed the north-facing windows. Leo admitted the space looked imposing, and his nerves tingled his shoulders.

"Can I help you?" a voice sounded from behind him in the doorway.

Leo spun around and saw one of the two women who he had just seen leave a moment earlier. As his mind caught up, he stuttered unintelligible sounds meant to be a greeting. "Are—sorry, I didn't mean—I'm looking for a Janice Masters, are you?"

The woman, with her caramel skin and dark hair, reminded him of America, only with an unamused face that terrified him. He supposed a good lawyer should have a good poker face, and this one did!

"I'm Ms. Masters," she said and hung her jacket on the coat tree in the corner. She came around the desk, cool as a cucumber, and sat in her leather chair. "And you are?"

"Really embarrassed," Leo said.

This made her crack a smile, for only a second, but he had seen it, and knew he could charm his way through the meeting if necessary.

"I've been waiting to see you all morning," Leo said and motioned to the chair across from her. "May I?" He didn't wait for her to answer, knowing it would be harder to kick him out if he was seated. He ignored her minor protest and continued. "I got an email last night from you—"

"Oh," she interrupted. "You're the mayor from Christmas Cove."

"You can call me Leo. And you can imagine the shock I've been in since last night."

"Leo, I was plain in my email. I'm sorry you waited for hours to talk to me, but there's nothing more I can do. It was a courtesy to inform you about the incorporation, nothing more," Masters said while scribbling something on a legal pad.

"Just like that? There's nothing we can do to save the town? I don't understand why we got notice today. It's only a week from now."

"The law is clear, Leo. It is an automatic trigger and happens at the end of the year. You simply don't have the requisite number of residents to stave off the incorporation."

"I thought we had more time. Another year." Leo ran his fingers through his hair while he considered a way forward. There was only one thing he thought could buy some time. "What about a full head count? On Christmas Eve, before the deadline, we gather the whole town and do a proper census. Are we allowed to do that?"

Ms. Masters sat back in her chair and tapped her pen against her lips as she thought about his question. She put a finger up to him and made her way to the bookshelves. A finger grazed across the spines and stopped on the one next to the last. Pulling out the book, she swiped pages to the left so fast, he couldn't count them.

"Here," she read the words for a moment and placed the book in front of him on the desk. "You, as Mayor, are allowed to appeal the decision and request a full count of the citizens of Christmas Cove. It looks like you have just over a week to assemble all legal residents inside your jurisdiction."

"Hope," he whispered and looked up at her. "I can't lose my town. It means everything to me. We'll have the numbers. Somehow. And Christmas Cove isn't going anywhere."

"I'll arrange for the magistrate to be there on Christmas Eve, before midnight. I can't promise you anything more than that." Ms. Masters put her hand out to him, and he stood. "Best of luck," she said.

"Thank you," Leo said.

With renewed passion for what they were doing in town, he walked out of the building. Bringing back Christmas had just taken on a whole new layer, and he wasn't going to be the bearer of unwelcome news and let the city down. He checked the time and hoped he wasn't too late.

There was exactly one person he wanted to confide in. One person who had the imagination and determination to right the train before it fell off the tracks totally. And if he hurried across town, he might just catch America before she left the library.

# CHAPTER 22

*THIS SHOULDN'T BE TOO HARD*, AMERICA TOLD HERSELF AS SHE pulled open the bakery's front door. She hadn't picked the particular establishment for any reason over another. It wasn't even the first shop on the street. But, as her tummy rumbled, she guessed at the cause. The smell of apples and nutmeg drifted to her nose and beckoned her inside. Espresso and pumpkin spice infused the air, and her mouth watered. Patrons filled the place to the brim, and a line stretched the length of the counter where small cakes, cookies decorated with icing and red and green sprinkles, and miniature pies sat behind the glass case.

There was nothing in Christmas Cove that could compete with this shop. Her high hopes for jumpstarting the beleaguered Cove were now buried under a mountain of self-doubt. Had Leo been right? Was she in over her head?

"Hi there, hon," a friendly face said from behind the counter. "I'll be right with you."

America nodded. *It would be a shame to not delight in Elizabethtown's Christmas offerings*, she thought as she examined the menu.

"What'll it be?" the same woman asked. Her bright blonde hair glittered in the light from the hundreds of mini lights that hung along the ceiling. Her rosy cheeks reminded her of Mrs. Claus, and America couldn't help but like the woman.

"I'll have an apple spice macchiato to go please," America said.

"Anything to eat with that?" the woman shifted her eyes to the case and back up to America.

"I'm not from here," America said. "Tell me, what's your favorite?"

Without a hesitation, the woman snapped her fingers and said, "One snickerdoodle croissant it is. I'll get you squared away. I'm Anne, by the way."

The patrons, standing shoulder to shoulder in the line, scooted America down the counter towards the register at the rear of the long store. "It's nice to meet you. I'm America."

As Anne worked, she spoke. "Where are you visiting from, America?"

"I'm actually staying nearby, in Christmas Cove."

Anne froze for a moment. "That's nice. I haven't been there for years. They used to have this bonfire every year—"

"We had it last night, actually," America interrupted.

"I hadn't realized," Anne turned towards America with the coffee and a small brown bag, "that the town was still putting on such events."

"That's actually why I'm here, in Elizabethtown today." America handed Anne a flier. "Christmas Cove is open for business again. I'm trying to get the word out, and thought I might hang this flier in your window and leave a pile for your guests too?" Her words were a statement presented as an unsure request.

Anne took the flier and considered it for a moment. "It would be nice to see the place again. Is it all decked out this year?"

"Pretty much," America said and smiled a little too wide to be convincing.

"Well, I don't see that it'll hurt anything. You can leave some here," Anne said. "That'll be seven dollars."

"I really appreciate this," America said. She placed a stack of fliers beside the register and handed Anne a ten note. "Keep the change. Merry Christmas."

"Merry Christmas to you too."

With her coffee and a delicious-looking croissant in one hand, and her fliers in the other, America skipped out of the bakery with a new zeal pushing her along. She only hoped the rest of the people would be as accepting as Anne had been. She handed fliers to anyone she passed on the sidewalk and ducked into several more establishments, meeting with mixed receptions, along her way.

One owner of a little toy shop said he wouldn't promote his competition, while another said, "What's the point? That town is dead." These revelations didn't help, and her mood soured more than she liked, but she was satisfied that the pile of fliers in her hand was nearly gone. She turned and looked back down the Main Street, lined with flocked trees and red ornaments, and saw that it was far more festive looking than what she'd been able to achieve, even with all the work they'd done in bringing the Cove up to par for the season.

She sighed and took a deep breath, wishing to speak to her parents. They always knew the right things to say, but never lied to her about the realities she faced. Checking her cell reception and the time, she figured the hour where her parents were staying in Italy. They would probably be out to dinner, and . . . no, she decided not to disturb them.

It was important that she go on by herself. She had some research to do at the library and needed to send her notes to Mr. Janowitz. The library was just ahead. It wasn't hard to miss its 1970s modern lines and concrete columns holding up a slanted, flat roof and topped with a large neon sign above the door.

Inside, the library smelled like the archives room at her office. Old paper mixed with the acidic tinge of the new. Fluorescent lights gave the whole space a cool, green tint that was off-putting and would ensure no one would linger too long in the space.

"Can I help you?" a young man said from behind a semi-circular counter centered on the front doors.

"Yes," she said. "I'm looking for some historical texts about Christmas Cove. And do you have free wifi?"

"Sure do," he said and pointed to a plastic placard on the counter that featured the wifi password. "There's a local section upstairs. Whatever we have will be up there."

She thanked the librarian and proceeded up the floating steps to the second floor. The area was no more than a loft where short bookcases and filing cabinets lined the walls. A low, round utility table, the sort one would find in an elementary school, sat in the middle of the space, and a water fountain grumbled in the corner.

The books were arranged by topic and author. There was no section specifically about Christmas Cove, but she found a couple of old almanacs and surveys of the county. The survey caught her attention. The maps were of particular interest since she had no real idea of the cove's size and shape, having only seen it empty and fogged over. The filing cabinets held a collection of county newspapers and were arranged by year. Their stories and photographs collected over the years could prove especially useful. Where a book is a big picture, a newspaper is a snapshot of a moment in time, and is less tainted by history's narrative.

Before the storm, the cove was at its finest. So, she began there. Looking back only a few years, she pulled a November issue. "Christmas Cove Elects New Mayor. Outsider brings inheritance to buy his way into position." A photo of Leo wearing a broad smile and standing in front of the fountain in the plaza sat below the headline. The story was curiously written and affected a negative view of the new mayor. She wondered who would care so much about the mayor of a tiny town to write such a smearing article in the first place.

Wanting something older, she put the issue back in its place in the file cabinet and flipped back to a December issue from a couple of years earlier. She spread the paper across the child-size table and kneeled down. Photos from a tree lighting and a schedule of events were plastered across the front page. The tree was easily twice the size of the one they had erected the day before, and the turnout looked to be in the hundreds, unlike the dozen or so that had attended their impromptu lighting and Edwin's musical entertainment.

A lantern lighting, ice fishing competition, and a fruit cake walk were all on the week's schedule. A snowman-making race and a hand-maker's market capped off the week's festivities before Christmas. The traditions she had seen advertised in the online brochure were all but forgotten now.

"We can't do the fishing," she said as she flipped through the pages. "No lake. No ice. And we can't do the snowman race since there's no snow. And . . ." America folded the paper and tossed it away from herself. "What's the point?"

Out the window, she saw all of Elizabethtown's Main Street, with its decorations and cheer. It looked like the place she should be covering for the magazine, and not the town that had forgotten what Christmas really means.

It didn't take America long to pull her mental notes together in a makeshift narrative and send them off. She made sure to include the history of Christmas Cove and the tragedy of the dam breaking. But one question lingered in her mind. Why would the mayor want a travel magazine to do a story about a place on its death bed?

"Ahem."

She tossed her head around, and her breath caught at the sight of a terribly upset Leo standing at the top step. His eyes narrowed, and he sucked shallow breaths through his pursed lips.

"Leo, what are you doing here? Are you okay?" she said and didn't even attempt to mask her concern. She was on her feet and walking towards him.

"Pa told me where to find you," he said and took both of her hands in his.

"You're not sick?"

He shook his head. "Sorry I lied to you. I just needed—"

"It's fine," she reassured, knowing his lie was half her fault. "What's going on? You look as though you just ran a mile."

"I did," he said. "Do you remember when I told you that there was more going on in the Cove than just the lake being gone?"

She nodded and searched his expression for understanding.

"There were rumors that we, Christmas Cove, would be incorporated into a bigger township if the population numbers dipped too low. And . . . they did, they have. I thought we had another year, or at least a year once the population dropped below the threshold, before the incorporation would take effect. I've been at the county lawyer's office for hours now, trying to figure out if there's any way to stop it."

"What does this mean? No more Christmas Cove?" America asked.

"Not as we know it, no."

"Unless what? What do you need to do?"

"I've filed an appeal, which means the state will perform a formal head count. We have until Christmas Eve to have a population of one hundred fifty permanent residents. Or else, the state law automatically kicks in and the town becomes part of Elizabethtown."

"Oh," she said and dropped his hands. "I see." Guilt dripped off of her. Only a moment earlier, she had dreamed of covering an Elizabethtown Christmas for the magazine and how much more interesting it looked than the Cove. "How can I help?" she said, but not out of guilt, out of a genuine desire not to see Leo in pain.

"Want to move in?" he said with a chuckle and roll of his eyes. "I can't believe I just asked you that."

She paced around the table and ducked a little on the far side where the roof slanted downward, though she wasn't in danger of hitting her head. "That's not a bad idea."

"Really?" he said, crimson lighting his cheeks.

"Not me necessarily, but maybe other people would move here if they knew," America said and rubbed her hands together as though they were cold. She checked her watch and saw the date. "We don't have much time, but I'm sure there are others who, like you, have fond memories of coming to the Cove. Maybe they would move here."

"In a week? The week before Christmas?" Leo questioned her idea and ran his hands back through his hair. "There's no way!"

"So, that's it? You're giving up on the town that you love?" Her words sounded harsher coming out than she had intended. How he flustered her so much, she would have to think about later.

"I'm not giving up. I just don't know what to do. And plus,

would it be so bad after all? It's not like the town is thriving, if you know what I mean," he said, and his phone rang. He looked at the screen. "It's the lawyer. I need to take this. Will you meet me downstairs in a few?"

America nodded. She had a few items to put away properly, and a phone call to make of her own.

# CHAPTER 23

THOUGH THE CHANCE OF HER MOTHER OR FATHER ANSWERING the phone was low, America hoped they had called it an early evening in whatever Italian city they were currently exploring. The phone rang a fourth and then fifth time before beeping over to voicemail.

"Hi, Mom. I hope you're having a good trip, and I can't wait to hear all about it in a few days when you get back," America began in a shaky voice. She cleared her throat and continued. "Things here have been crazy, and I could really use your advice about something. I'm fine. So, don't worry, but you may not be able to contact me if you try and call me back.

"I'm not in the city. The magazine sent me on assignment to a little place called Christmas Cove, up north. I'm supposed to draft an article about the idyllic holiday vacation spot, but things aren't going well here. Anyway. The town is in some legal trouble since there aren't enough residents, and the neighboring town will incorporate the whole area if they don't have enough people by the twenty-fourth.

"To complicate things more. I've become somewhat

invested in the outcome here. It's probably a good case study on why I should not be a writer, and stick to editing." America looked at her watch. The message had already gone on for too long and she would likely be cut off at any moment. "Anyway, Mom, I was hoping Dad might have some legal advice or know someone who could help. Email me back if you get this, since I don't have much reception here. I love you."

The phone beeped and cut out.

America sat back down at the low table and opened her computer. She sent off a few photos to her mom before drafting an email to her boss.

*Dear Mr. Janowitz,*

*I've just learned some disturbing news about Christmas Cove that you will want to include. The Cove doesn't have enough people to support itself, and will soon be incorporated into a neighboring township. The city only needs a few new residents. I can get you the exact number later.*

*Sir, we must do something to get the word out or the town will die. If there is any way you can help, any bulletin you can put out in the newsletter or on social, that would be wonderful. Again, I'm not available to speak until I get back to the city, but please see if there is anything you can do. You know I would not ask such a big favor if it weren't important to me, and to the people of Christmas Cove.*

*Sincerely,*

*America Greene*

She hit send and closed the computer, unsure if anything would materialize from her appeals.

With a buoyancy to her steps, she hastened down the stairs and out the door, where Leo was pacing in front of an iron bench. He held the phone against his ear, and she thought she spied a tiny smile hidden behind his forearm.

"Good news," he said and ended the call. He slid the

phone into his jacket pocket and shook his head. "Jenny Townsend just had her baby."

"That's fantastic," America said. "One down . . ."

"Would you believe it? The baby came two weeks early, and just in time," he said as though he didn't believe it himself.

"How many more people do you need, exactly?"

"Five."

"That's not many at all! How hard can it be to find five more people to move here?" she wondered aloud, though she should have kept it to herself by the look on Leo's face.

Leo turned to face her straight on and put his arms out. He wanted a hug. He needed a hug from her. She allowed him to embrace her for a long moment, and his muscles relaxed a little.

While pressed together, he whispered in her ear, "I appreciate your optimism and how much you want to help, America. But I really think this is a done deal." He stepped back from her. "I want to go home. Will you ride with me?"

# CHAPTER 24

"Stop the truck!" America yelled.

Leo slammed on the brakes and pulled over near the sidewalk. "What is it?" he shouted.

"I have a great idea."

"Slow your roll, America. You have *an* idea. Let's decide later if it's a great one," Leo joked.

It felt nice to hear him jest. After the bonfire, she wasn't sure if he could be that free with her again. She still needed to find time to talk things out, but with the dire news of him about to lose the city, she put their personal talk on the back burner.

Shuffling down the street ahead of them, Carol waved a frantic hand. She looked as though she wanted to see them as much as America wanted to see Carol.

America turned to Leo and took his face in her hands. "Who loves this place more than you do?" she asked. His blank stare frustrated her, and she pointed out the front windshield at the old woman walking towards them.

"Carol?" he said. "What's your point?"

"She knows everyone in town, and she will want to help us when we tell her what's going on with the town takeover," America said and used the crank inside the door to lower the window. "Carol!" she yelled at the window and waved her over, though Carol was already making a beeline towards the truck. "Do you have a minute?"

"You're the bright faces I wanted to see," she said. "Here, I made a fresh batch." Carol handed over a plate of gingerbread cookies. "I thought you two could enjoy these . . . together."

*Did she really wink?,* America thought and bit back a giggle at the woman's not-so-slick prodding, but appreciated Carol's effort. She peeled the cling wrap from the plate and the cab filled with a sweet scent from the cookies.

"Might as well," Leo said. A side grin and a quick glance let America know that he was all right and seeing clearly past the shocking news of the day.

"Thank you very much for the cookies, Carol. I'm sure we'll enjoy these," America said. "Now, we have something to tell you. We've just come from Elizabethtown, and Leo learned that the Cove will be incorporated into their town if there aren't enough people living here."

This information was an obvious surprise to the woman, who held her hand over her chest and played with the gold chain at her neck. "I did not know that. I mean, I heard rumors, but—are you certain, Leo?"

He nodded. "We have until Christmas Eve to get six more permanent residents. Well, five now. Jenny Townsend had her baby this morning."

Carol clapped her hands. "What wonderful news. I should bring some cookies over to the Townsend place later."

"I'm sure that would be appreciated," America said at the sweet idea.

Leo, oblivious to what Carol had said, continued. "I just don't see any way we can pull it off. But America was just about to tell me her plan."

America certainly did. She had already reached out to her boss at the magazine, and to her parents, though that avenue was a longshot. Carol could help get the word out. And there was always Poppy's talent at being three steps ahead of everyone else—certainly there some way she could help too.

Meanwhile, Leo need not know the lengths she was willing to go to help save the town. Until something panned out, anyway. There was no use in getting his hopes up unnecessarily.

"I can make some calls," Carol said with a worried smile. "I'll do what I can and let you know if I make any progress. If that's what you really want, Leo?"

"It's one thing when we were just putting out some decorations and celebrating Christmas again. But this? It's too much. I'm sorry if I'm letting you down as your mayor. I simply don't have the answer, but any help you can give me can't hurt."

America put her hand on his knee. Admitting one's pride must be hard for any man, let alone one that had as kind a heart as Leo did. There was no reason to make him feel worse about the situation than he already did. As the scope of what had to be done became clear, his forced smile and wet eyes threatened to break her heart, and she squeezed his knee to let him know she was there.

"Thank you, Carol." America said. "For the treats and for your help. My mouth is already watering. These cookies smell delicious."

"Good luck, you two," she said and turned to leave.

America held a cookie in front of Leo's nose and waved it about. "You want a bite?"

With a small nod, he leaned over and bit a chunk from the gingerbread cookie still in her hand. Crumbs fell all over the seat between them, and she brushed them to the floorboard before scooting a couple of inches closer to him.

Leo licked the edge of his mouth but missed a crumb clinging to his upper lip. America swiped her thumb across it. "Better?" Her question was so much deeper than just the crumb. Wrapped in her words and calming smile were a dozen more ways she hoped he was better. She wanted him to be happy. She wanted all the hurt in his life to be better.

"Thank you," Leo said. A soft kiss landed on her forehead, and her eyes closed for a moment. "I don't know how I would be doing if you weren't here with me right now."

"I'm glad I'm helping and not making things harder for you."

"Don't get me wrong," he chuckled, "you're definitely making things more complicated for me. But not harder."

America considered what he was saying. Was she complicating his quiet life in the country too much? Was she disturbing the equilibrium of the small town in ways she hadn't considered simply by being there?

"You're complicating things for me too, you know?" she said, though she hadn't realized until that moment, sitting with a man she had never planned on meeting, who rapidly and wholly becoming the focus of her thoughts, that he was someone worth complicating things for.

Somehow, they had driven all the way back to the cabin without her taking notice. The day was fading, and she had no idea what the next day would hold for each of them.

"Leo," she began to say, just as he said her name at the same time.

"You go ahead." Leo parked the truck and turned the radio on. A country singer, who she didn't recognize but whose twang was unmistakable as any other genre, sang a rendition of The Christmas Song.

"No, you go first," she said.

"I just want to thank you for sparking joy in this town again. No matter what happens next," Leo said while wringing his hands on the leather steering wheel. "Now, what were you going to say?"

America was unsure if this was the right moment, but with her deadline looming over her to write a great article, the future of Christmas Cove teetering on the unknown, and her swelling affections for the man sitting beside her, she decided to go with her gut.

"I was wondering . . . what I mean to say is, when I was in the town that shall remain nameless—"

"You can say it. Elizabethtown."

"Elizabethtown. I saw there was a dance tomorrow night."

"Countyline Christmas?"

"Yes." America clapped and rubbed her fingers together. "I was wondering if you—"

"Stop right there, America."

America began to protest, but closed her lips tightly. She shifted away from him from embarrassment and grabbed the door handle to leave.

Leo's hand covered hers on the latch and pulled her back towards himself. She locked eyes with him and searched for his meaning through the confusion in her mind.

"America, would you like to accompany me to the Countyline Christmas dance tomorrow evening?" Leo said with a smirk.

"Yes. I would love to go with you."

"I haven't danced in quite a while. These boots might be a little rusty," Leo warned.

"I think you'll be all right."

"Pick you up at seven?"

America nodded and opened the door, afraid that if she looked back at Leo again, she would want to stay right where she was, beside him. "See you then," she said and made for the cabin's front door.

# CHAPTER 25

Leo got nearly zero sleep that night. After dropping America at the cabin, he proceeded to his home a couple miles away. Laying in the dark, with only a few stars to light his window, his mind tossed between the two things tugging at his heart: America and the Cove.

How had America breezed into his life, into his town, and shaken him so? Her dark hair and joyful eyes teased him, but she also made him feel hopeful and not alone anymore.

But her time in Christmas Cove was temporary. He had known that from the start. She was on assignment, one that didn't include falling in love with the mayor. He was certain that wasn't on the agenda. But there was something in how she looked at him, how at-ease they were with each other, how she pushed him outside his quiet and uneventful comfort zone, and how he wanted to be with her always, that told him not to take the chance meeting with her for granted.

Could he ask her to stay?

If he did, would she even want to?

These were questions he needed an answer to before he allowed his heart to form any new connections to her. The dance was the perfect setting for him to gauge her true feelings.

But Leo was dealing with so much more than just a crush on the city girl.

Even with the biggest and most over-the-top Christmas celebration that he and America could pull together, there was little chance the Cove would magically get enough residents by the deadline.

Everything changed since hearing the news of the incorporation. He was the mayor. The only mayor the Cove had, and the only person standing in the breach against the takeover, and he knew he was in over his head. His last-ditch attempt to bring back Christmas and stop his town from dying all together was feeble at best, and foolish at worst.

He and America had gotten the town's hopes up, their joy was starting to return, and things felt less gray than they had only days earlier. The change was evident on Main Street, where the neighbors had put out even more decorations and lights. There were more twinkling lights and shiny ornaments than he'd seen for a long time. Did those people think it was a fool's errand?

With the hours ticking by, Leo had a choice to make. He could put everything into finding a way to save the Cove, or he could let the takeover go ahead.

Would it be so bad if Elizabethtown facilitated the necessary functions of the city? The Cove would always be the Cove, even if it was a tiny corner of an empty lake turned grassy plain. They could still have Christmas their way. They could revitalize with new industry, like becoming a retreat destination, just like he and Pa had discussed.

Leo spent the day in his drafty office at the town hall, making phone calls and scouring old contracts, looking for any way out of the agreement with Elizabethtown. His eyeballs felt like they were bleeding from having read so many legal documents. After hours and hours, he was no closer to a solution than he had been the day before.

He needed a break, and seven o'clock couldn't come fast enough.

The black antique phone rang at his desk.

"Hello?"

"When exactly were you planning on telling me about the incorporation?" a voice Leo knew all too well scolded.

"Hi, Pa. Who told you?"

"It doesn't matter. What matters is that I'm calling to find out what the plan is," Edwin said, as though he was answering to a superior officer.

The old man's tone made Leo pause. He *was* in command of the situation. He was the mayor, and it was high time he started acting like it.

"So far, I've made no headway with finding a way out of the contract between Elizabethtown and the Cove. The agreement was automatically triggered when the population dropped below one fifty. As far as I can see, we have to beat the population threshold in time, or . . ." Leo's alternative was the least appealing option, but a viable one if he was willing to swallow a big piece of humble pie.

"Go on," Edwin urged.

"Or I somehow get Elizabethtown to agree to not pursue the incorporation further."

Through the phone line, Leo could hear Edwin tapping his fingers as he considered the options. A deep breath and a throaty grunt came before his words. "Option two isn't going to happen, is it?"

"I would like to avoid that one, if possible, but it may be the only way," Leo said and swallowed hard. "Let's hope it doesn't come to that."

"And in the meantime?"

"Carol said she would contact some of her old friends and

maybe convince some of them to move back to town. America said she had some ideas today." Leo checked the wooden clock hanging on the wall. "I've got to go. I don't want to be late."

"Got a hot date tonight?" Edwin asked in a playful tone.

"As a matter of fact—"

"Where are you taking the city girl?"

"How do you know I'm going on a date with America?"

"Oh, come on. Everyone can see how your eyes get all googly when she's nearby," Edwin chuckled. "Now, where are you all going?"

"Countyline Christmas," Leo answered as he put his coat on one arm. "I have to go. Let's talk tomorrow."

Leo hung up and dashed out the door. On the way to the cabin, Leo swung by his house and changed his more casual plaid shirt to a crisp white one. He pulled a red sweater over his head and combed his hair back before dabbing some old cologne on his neck.

Leo didn't know what to expect when he pulled his truck up to the cabin, but he was not expecting to see America waiting on the front porch for him. His headlights illuminated her like a spotlight hitting a stage. She glittered like frost in a silver gown that hung to the floor. He took a deep breath and exited the cab, suddenly wishing he had a nicer vehicle to pick her up in.

America glowed as she turned a slow turn. "How do I look?"

Leo had never seen a more beautiful sight. He approached slowly to take her in. Her lips were painted red like cranberries, and her eyes twinkled against the sparkly dress. Her hair was pinned up in soft curls at the crown of her head. He was certain he was blushing as she extended a hand to him.

Taking her delicate fingers in his hand, he drew her near and kissed the back of her hand. "You are incredible." Leo took a ringlet hanging along the side of her face and twirled it around his finger while thinking about how he was wrapped around hers. He would do anything to keep her.

"You clean up nicely too." America cracked a smile and motioned for him to twirl as she had just done.

Leo chuckled, but complied with her request, even batting his eyelashes as he came around to face her again. His effort was worth seeing her smirk with a small bite of her lower lip in response to his silliness.

"Are you ready to dance?" she said and slipped her arm through the crook of his elbow.

"Yes ma'am," Leo said and clicked his boot heels together.

He escorted her across the drive and held her dress as she climbed into his old truck. The drive was short, a nice walk to take during warmer weather, but not while wearing a long silver gown. He glanced at her, and back at the road, about a dozen times while on the way. She caught him on more than one occasion and smiled wider each time.

Once they arrived at the dance, Leo led her into the pavilion. The wooden structure, situated on the border of two counties, and hemmed in by train tracks on one side, and the river on the other, was a favorite destination for love birds and birdwatchers alike. Although Leo couldn't recall a time when he had ever taken a girl there on a date.

Leo watched as America's eyes lit up. The space was a winter wonderland, complete with dozens of flocked and lit trees. Soft glowing faux candles dotted the room, a live band played at one end, and there was more punch and hot cocoa than one could drink.

"This is beautiful," America said as she took in the atmosphere.

"You're beautiful," he whispered. Though he couldn't see if she heard him, her shoulder moved ever so slightly as though she did. "Is this the Christmas you were hoping for?"

"Close," she said and took a turn around him while delighting in the moment.

America looked like the queen of the ball as they walked to the center of the space, and pride swelled inside Leo that she was on his arm. The crowd hushed and, as though they were witnessing something special, cleared room on the dancefloor.

Though they didn't know who she was, her confident and relaxed posture commanded attention from everyone in the room. She sent Leo a knowing side glance as he twirled her around before catching her in his arm.

He took her left hand in his and her waist in his right. The room stood still in the breath just before the music began. A Christmas waltz. Leo knew this one well. He took her through the steps, and she followed his lead like a pro.

As the music swelled and diminished to a close, he captured her gaze. She radiated happiness.

"Where did you learn to dance like that?" America said breathlessly.

"YouTube."

America whacked him in the belly as she laughed. "You did not!"

He liked teasing her. "Of course I didn't. My Aunt June insisted on weekly cotillion classes."

"You surprise me."

"I try," Leo said and held her close.

Her arms draped over his shoulders and her head rested near his neck. "Thank you," she whispered. "This is exactly what I imagined before I came here."

"You imagined dancing with a dashing, yet approachable public servant in a snow-themed pavilion with a hundred eyes trained on you while your favorite song is played by a live band, while wearing a stunning gown and falling madly in—"

"Yes," America answered with no hint of hesitation in her voice, which surprised him.

They had only just met days ago, and couldn't possibly have such big feelings, let alone talk about it. Leo held her closer at her waist. America's breath caught ever so slightly at the change in proximity between them. She melted into his embrace as the music permeated the air around them. A crisp chill blew in, and he covered her exposed back with his hands. He felt her tremble under his touch.

In that moment, he didn't care what happened to the town. He didn't care about anything other the woman in his arms and making her happy.

"What do you want for Christmas, America?"

"What do you mean?"

"If you could have anything you want." Leo spoke quietly near her ear as though they were sharing secrets. He hoped she would say she wanted to be with him.

"Well, if I could have anything? I want my article to do well, and I want my parents to get back safely from Italy," she said. "Why? What about you?"

What about him? He knew he wanted her, but fear seized his tongue. And his nerve. "I want you . . . to get everything you want. That's it."

"You don't want the Cove to be saved?" she asked and backed away a little.

Uncomfortable with his momentary neglect of the town, he shook his head. "Of course, I want that. I just don't know what to do about the Cove. And this, me and you, is so much easier than dealing with the hard stuff."

"Can I ask you something?" America spoke while rocking back and forth in time with the music. "I know you moved here so that you could stay connected to the memory of your parents, but after the dam broke, why weren't you willing to work hard enough and do what it takes to keep the magic alive?"

Her words hit a little too close to the truth. His hands dropped and hung loose at his side while he felt his defenses going up. "You don't know what you're talking about, America."

"I know what I see. I'm not blind to the fact that you have done nothing to keep the Christmas in Christmas Cove, or else it wouldn't have taken a stranger with zero resources to come here and make things happen. You could have done this years ago, and you didn't." America took a breath long enough to grab a glass of prosecco from a waiter's tray and down it before continuing. "I think you like the pity, but you need to snap out of it before you lose everything."

"America, I . . . I . . ." It was Leo's turn to down a glass of prosecco.

"There's something I don't understand. Why did you want the magazine to come here in the first place?"

"Me?" Leo began. Confusion twisted his face.

"Yes, you!" America's ringtone, "The Twelve Days of Christmas", cut the air between them. She dug in her small clutch and pulled out the phone.

He had never been less happy for a good signal. It was the second time she had insinuated that he had asked the magazine to come there, and the second time his answer was interrupted. They had a lot more to talk to about, and now it would have to wait.

"It's my boss. I have to take this," America said and walked towards the entrance of the pavilion furthest from the bandstand.

What did she mean about him wanting the magazine to write about the Cove? He had never even thought of it, though he wished he would have years ago. It could have saved the town from losing so much.

SARAH DRESSLER

Before America arrived, he had even thought of opening the Cove as a retreat destination all year round. And during the cold months, bringing back the festivals and traditions that the Cove had always been known for.

But requesting a travel magazine to feature the town's Christmas celebrations when there was nearly none to speak of was not his idea. But whose?

# CHAPTER 26

AMERICA COULDN'T GET OUT THE DOOR FAST ENOUGH WHEN she answered the call.

"Hello, America Greene speaking,"

"America, I'm so glad I caught you," Mr. Janowitz said. "I hope I'm not interrupting anything."

America looked back inside and spotted Leo's tousled blond hair over the top of the crowd. He ran his fingers through his waves and turned in circles, kicking the floor as she'd seen him do before.

"You have perfect timing," America said. "What can I do for you, sir?"

"I finally got to reading those notes you sent over yesterday. I apologize for not calling earlier in the day. I think it's great. You have a knack for capturing the heart of a story."

"Thank you," America said shyly, unaccustomed to hearing feedback on her writing prowess.

"I think we have everything we need for the article. Great work, America." Janowitz said. "Seeing as your assignment is done, I was hoping you would come back to the city early. You're still my best editor and there's quite a bit of work to do on some of the other articles. I know you were supposed to be there for another few days, but I don't see any reason you should stay."

She paused, considering the man who she was falling for and the comfortable life she had waiting for her back in the city.

"America, you can stay if you want, the trip is paid for, but based on your notes, I doubt there's anything left for you there. Why don't you come on back. We can polish up your story and you can enjoy the rest of the holiday season back at home."

A cold wind blew past America and chilled her arms. A train rounded the bend and tooted its whistle as it began to cross a small bridge over the creek running near the pavilion. Inside, Leo was standing beside the food table and talking to an older couple. His eyes scanned beyond their heads for a moment before returning back to the woman speaking to him.

"I don't think there's anything more I can do here." America said. "I'm glad you like the article."

America hung up the phone and checked the time on her wristwatch. The time didn't matter, all she knew was that her time was up in Christmas Cove.

She found Leo and asked him to take her back to the cabin. "I need to go home," she said. "My boss says I'm done here."

"Are we?" Leo asked with a stitch of hurt cracking his low voice.

America turned and walked towards his truck without acknowledging his question. It was too painful to think about their budding relationship being nipped so stupidly in the bud. They were each to blame. His high expectations for what love was supposed to look like as compared to his parents' perfect love, his hiding and not trying to save the

Cove until she turned up and forced his hand, and her pushing, always pushing, for more.

During the ride back to the cabin, she said nothing. He said nothing, though their eyes met a few times, the silence between them spoke more than any words could have.

She got out of the truck and slowly closed the door, wondering whether she should say something—an apology for insulting his motives and his lack of action, for kicking him when he was down. Or was she hoping he would say something to her? He said nothing. Did nothing.

As she stood frozen in her own disappointment at the way things were ending between them, he pulled out of the drive. A dust cloud mingled with the night air and the truck disappeared over the crest.

"Dang," America said and kicked every rock in her path up to the cabin door.

How could she be so stupid, and what right did she have to accuse Leo of hiding, of not caring about his town? Inside, she closed the door and flopped on the sofa in front of the little tree. A pool of silver fabric fell like a waterfall down the sofa to the floor. America threw her small bag on the coffee table as an exasperated sigh hissed through her teeth and echoed against the wooden walls.

America fiddled with her phone, flipping it into the air, and catching it again as she took stock of what she had done. She had stormed into town and left chaos in her wake. It was so uncharacteristic of her, and yet, she had never felt as passionate about a project as she did about bringing Christmas back to Christmas Cove. Her motivations may have been selfish at the start. She just wanted to have something worthwhile to write about. But the Cove had changed her in more ways than she cared to admit, least of all the way her heart now ached for its mayor.

A pit opened in her stomach. Was she really done? Was

this it? She knew she wasn't cut out to be a full-time writer, but now she questioned her aptitude for knowing when to keep her mouth shut, too. She had been an unmitigated fool. There was certainly a better way to have spoken to Leo, and surely a better time.

Leo may be resigned to defeat, but she wasn't a quitter and had proclaimed that she had an idea, a way to save the Cove. The town still needed help, and she knew there was more she could do. Unlocking her phone, she pulled up Poppy's contact info and ran to the bedroom, where the landline phone sat on the small end table beside the bed.

She dialed and waited. No one picked up. Poppy was probably screening her calls, like America would have done. She dialed again. "Pick up. Pick up."

"Hello?" Poppy said.

"Poppy, it's America. I have a—"

"Oh, hi! I thought it might be you. Are you having a fun time on vacation, I mean, assignment?"

"No. I mean, I was. But I need your help."

Poppy must have heard the urgency in America's voice, and her tone dropped a whole octave. "Start at the beginning."

America regaled her friend and coworker with the details of her trip thus far. Poppy was quiet and listened to the whole tale, which America appreciated, though she was unsure whether she was listening out of obligation as her assistant, or as a devoted friend.

"Let me get this straight," Poppy said. "You fell in love with the mayor and then insulted his very being?"

"Seriously," America dropped back onto the bed. "That's what you got from all that?"

"Don't you think it's strange that you decided to stay in the first place? I mean, there were no Christmas festivities for you to cover. Don't you think Mr. Janowitz would have been happy to scrap the story at that point? No one would blame you. So, why *did* you stay?"

America had to think about it. Did she stay so that she could write her first article, or was she hooked when Leo showed up at the cabin with a tree that first morning? The truth was somewhere in the middle. "I stayed to spend more time with Leo. The holiday makeover was just the excuse, I suppose."

Butterflies swirled in her belly at having admitted it out loud. Was she falling in love with a man she had only just met? How could that be possible? One thing was sure, any feelings that he might have felt for her were gone now that she had been so cruel.

"So, what now?" Poppy asked.

Was she crying? America hadn't realized but wiped a tear from her cheek. "The people here, Pa and Carol—"

"And the mayor?"

"Yes, Leo too. I want them to have joy again," America said and eyed the Christmas tree sparkling out in the living area. "You know how much I love Christmas?"

"Everyone knows," Poppy said with a giggle.

"I can't bear knowing the namesake place has lost their Christmas spirit. I really thought I could help. But I was wrong. No trees, wreaths, or Christmas cookies alone can bring light back to the town. It was a selfish endeavor to want to make this place like it used to be, and all so I could spend time with that guy and draft the perfect article."

"Oh, America. It's not selfish at all," Poppy said. "All right, a little selfish. But you deserve to be happy in life, too."

"Janowitz says my draft is great as is and thinks I should come back to the city. Something in my gut is telling me that the story isn't over yet, but I'm going to come home anyway. I don't think there's much I can do here." With a fissure tearing through her heart, she pulled her suitcase from under the bed. "Can you see if there's a driver, or I'd even take the train in the morn—"

"Done," Poppy interrupted.

"What do you mean, done?"

"I have you booked on the 7:23 train out of Elizabeth-town. It'll be longer than the drive, but I will pick you up at the station before lunch, Are you certain you have no further business to take care of?"

America was absolutely in no way certain, but she was unable to see any other way forward. "Sometimes it's better to retreat and regroup. I'll see you tomorrow."

# CHAPTER 27

AMERICA PUSHED HER WAY OUTSIDE OF THE STATION DOOR where people hailed taxis and others excitedly greeted waiting family and friends. Steam filtered out from storm-grates along the curb, and the city's distinct briny scent hit her hard after spending so many days in the clean mountain air. Poppy's bright smile was a sight for America's weary eyes.

Poppy threw her arms around America's neck. "How was the trip back in? I talked to your property owner, and she said the apartment should be ready to move back into later today. So, for now, it's just you and me and whatever you want to do to waste time."

America could barely wrap her head around the onslaught of information and options. "My apartment? That's good," she said. "I hadn't even thought about it. You really are the best."

"I know," Poppy said in the way that America imagined a Barbie would speak if one could. "I'll get your bag. You get in and relax."

Poppy flopped into the driver's seat of the small purple

hatchback and pulled out into the heavy midday traffic while honking the horn and gesturing out the window with what looked to be an extended middle finger. "So, where to?"

America bit back a giggle at seeing her assistant so animated. There was only one place America could think of going. Only one place had the resources and minds she felt she needed to put things right again. "The office."

"Seriously? I thought you'd want to go out for a cup of coffee or those delicious pastries you always bring in to share with the staff. You know, you're the talk of the tenth floor?"

"I am?"

"They can't stop talking about the Cove. Mr. Janowitz told someone, and there was even a message board where people were taking bets on how this whole thing would pan out, if you know what I mean?"

"No, Poppy, I do not know what you mean!"

"It's possible that I added to Mr. Janowitz's story and told everyone about the guy."

"You didn't!" America felt vomit rising in her stomach. If there was one thing that she dreaded more than being late to something, was being the center of any kind of office drama. It was better for her as the editor to be trusted and neutral. Now what would people think?

"I didn't say anything about the almost kiss. But people figured it out pretty easily that there was way more going on at the Cove than just Christmassy things. Everyone thinks you are crazy for coming home instead of staying there and fixing things with him," Poppy said and switched lanes.

America didn't like highways. There were too many uncontrollable factors for her liking. By now, they were one exit away from their ramp, and then just two blocks more to the office. She took a deep breath and checked her watch. It had died. She supposed she had too much on her mind last night to plug it in.

"What's the plan when we get to the office?" Poppy asked. "I'm at your service."

"I know you are," America said.

"And not just because you pay my salary," Poppy added with a smile. "I really want you to be happy."

"Thanks, Poppy. Tell me, is it going to be bad for me in there?"

The hatchback screamed around the corner, and Poppy pulled right into an empty parking spot. America's nails dug into the side handle and her knuckles turned white. If she hadn't thrown up at the thought of everyone in the office knowing her business with Leo, she certainly thought about doing so now from Poppy's wild driving.

"It'll be fine. I promise. Just cover your head with your scarf and wear those big sunglasses you like. Also, stay low and crouch behind me. Piece of cake."

America nodded and donned her disguise, all the while feeling absurd. Poppy was bold, she had to give her that.

"Do you want to talk to the boss first?" Poppy asked.

"No. That won't be necessary. I need to get some things figured out. Does he know I'm coming?"

"America, everyone knows you're coming back, though they might be surprised to see you in the office today."

Being close to lunchtime, the office was nearly deserted. Lucky for them, they rode the elevator alone and made it down the long glass hallway to her office without so much as a look from another person, though she knew it was but a matter of time before she was found out. Knowing a confrontation was inevitable, she unwrapped herself and sat at her desk.

Poppy pulled up a chair on the opposite side and took out a notebook and a pile of colorful pens. "Hit me!"

America laughed at the rainbow explosion on her desk. "That's funny that you think I have any kind of a plan."

"You always have a plan. It's kind of your thing."

"Consider me reformed, then." America rocked back in her chair while she considered her next course of action.

"Let's start with the problem." Poppy opened her notebook and uncapped a red pen. On the top line, she drew a little holly berry as a bullet point. "You want Leo, but you screwed things up, and now you want to fix it, but you don't know how?"

"Don't write that!" America slapped her hand on the desktop. "And no. The problem is that Christmas Cove needs five more people to move in before Christmas Eve or the city will cease to exist."

"Could have fooled me," Poppy said under her breath.

"I heard that. And you aren't entirely wrong."

"Is there a way we can do both?"

"Both, huh?" There was no immediate reason that she shouldn't at least try. Even if the city were somehow saved, Leo deserved more than she'd given him at the dance. He was the kindest man she had ever met, and sexy as hell. He had gone out of his way to give her the sort of Christmas she expected, and she had given him nothing but dashed hopes and broken trust.

"Let's just say, hypothetically, that you get five more residents within the next week. Then what?" Poppy asked while she scribbled her ideas on the white pages.

"Pray that everything works out." America said. "And someday, who knows, Leo finds his match and lives happily ever after."

"I'm going to ignore your pity party for the moment and get to work on problem *numero uno*." Poppy slammed her notebook shut and put her hand out. "Give me all your notes."

America was taken aback by Poppy's demand and

promptly handed over her computer. "Everything you need is in the *C.Cove* folder on the desktop. It's not much."

"It'll be enough."

"Are you going to Mr. Janowitz now?"

"Not until I have something to add."

Poppy left the office and shut the door behind herself, leaving America in the quiet solitude of her own mind. Only, her brain wasn't quiet at all. How could she be so stupid? Falling for the mayor, and promptly sabotaging any hope of a relationship with him before she had a chance to tell him how she felt was not in the plan.

What she really wanted to do was to pick up the phone and call Leo. She wanted to apologize for her harsh words. Taking her cell phone from her pocket, America scrolled through her contacts to Leo's number. Her thumb hovered above his name. In truth, she didn't know what she would say, even if by some miracle the call actually went through and he picked up.

Poppy burst through the door, her red hair half falling from a claw clip on her crown and sporting a wide smile. "I've got it!"

"What did you get, Poppy?"

"Here." She placed the laptop in front of America and opened the screen. "I wrote a kind of 'wanted' ad for Christmas Cove. I'm putting it in the teaser for next week's issue that'll go out tomorrow." She stood over America's shoulder. "I figured, after all that stuff you said about how great Christmas Cove used to be, that somewhere, there might be a few people who want to move back."

"I had that same thought," America sighed and shut the screen. "I just don't think that someone can pick up their whole life and move on such short notice. I appreciate this, though."

"Well . . ." Poppy took the laptop. "Since you don't have a

better idea, I'm sending this out anyway. It can't hurt. Plus. I thought that if Leo saw how hard you were trying to help, that he might. I don't know . . . forgive you?" she shrugged.

"You're right. It won't hurt anything. Thank you, Poppy."

"You know, in all the time I've known you, I've never seen you so unsure. You're different. Like somehow you left a piece of yourself behind in that town, or with its mayor," Poppy teased.

America didn't respond. She did feel changed. For the first time in her adult life, she understood what it really meant to want someone else's happiness more than her own. Leo was kinder to her than she deserved. Even following her embarrassing plea to leave as soon as she had gotten to town, he had only thought of her needs and wants, and delivered to her a Christmas tree of her very own, while she had only wanted out.

If it weren't for the tiny tree in the corner of the living area, decorated with one strand of mini lights and a few ornaments, she would have left and never looked back. Closing her eyes, she pictured the cabin in her mind, walking around the sofa and plopping down with a glass of white in her hand, Leo knocking on the door.

Knocking on the door? Her eyes flew open at the sound. Behind the glass, Mark stood holding a plate of cookies wrapped in red cellophane with a ribbon tied around. As she looked distantly at the tall, forty-something with gray speckled hair and bushy brows, she couldn't remember why she had ever liked him in the first place. The memory of swooning whenever he would come by or pay her a compliment seemed a million miles away now.

She motioned for him to enter. "Are those for me?"

His brow knitted together and formed one large caterpillar across his forehead as though he had no idea of what she was talking about.

"The cookies?" she said.

He looked down at the object in his hands and tilted his head. *Did he even know he had been carrying the plate?* she wondered. Her head followed his cocked gaze and then righted again.

"Oh, these. No. Someone left them in the break room, and I figured they were for me."

"Why would you think that?" she asked and bit back a laugh.

"People are always leaving little gifts for me around the office," he said with no hint of awareness.

"Are you certain that you aren't just taking things that don't belong to you?" America asked.

He seemed to ponder the idea for a moment and then grinned. "Nope."

For the first time, she saw the man as he truly was. Daft. Handsome, completely unaware of his privilege, yet somehow utterly self-absorbed. Infatuation is a funny thing that distorts the world around it. If obsession twists one's thinking, then it was also possible that all the feeling she had for Leo were a lie.

The butterflies fluttering in her belly told a different story. Leo made her feel excited and happy, and she couldn't remember the last time she had felt so free with her time or heart. She knew now that she had never felt any of that for Mark. In fact, she had never felt anything for him personally. She realized that it was his confident demeanor and his friendly vibes that she had been in awe of, not to mention his engaging writing skills.

Her admiration could find a place to stay, but in that moment, she simply let go of the fangirl she had once been.

"What can I do for you, Mark?" America packed up her bag and grabbed her coat as she spoke.

"I was seeing if the rumors are true," he said and moved

out of her way as she passed through the doorway. "You fell in love with the mayor?"

There was no point in lying to him. He would spread whatever rumor he wanted to after the encounter. "Yep. Hook, line, and sinker. The mayor was marvelous." She shimmied her shoulders for effect and walked towards the elevator. Mark followed a few steps and must have realized he was being toyed with. His footsteps stopped their pursuit as she got in the lift. Turning, she watched him curiously and waved her fingers as the door shut.

# CHAPTER 28

THE LAST HALF FLIGHT OF STAIRS IN AMERICA'S APARTMENT building always felt like twice as many as the first six floors did. She trudged up the remaining steps as though she was on a climbing expedition. The whole place smelled like stale bread, as though the doors had been shuttered for way longer than a week. As soon as she stepped into her apartment, she planned to make straight for the windows and flood the place with some fresh, albeit city air. She jiggled her keys and listened for the one with the highest pitch *ting*, which was her apartment key.

From under her door, a thin ribbon of light spilled into the hallway. She questioned whether she had left a light on, or the drapes open, in her rush to get to the worst first writing assignment in the history of writing assignments. She turned the knob and nudged the door open with her toe.

Inside, her perfectly decorated Christmas tree and its hundreds of twinkling lights was turned on, though she distinctly recalled feeling sad when she had darkened the lights before leaving. The tree should not have been on.

"Hello?" she called out and noticed light coming from the kitchen too.

America, hot from the climb and the unseasonably warm weather, dropped her coat from her arm and hung her bag on the hook above the bench situated beside the door. Not only were all her lights on, but the air also smelled like lemon cleaner and . . . *Cranberries?* she wondered.

A cackle, which could only be her mother's laugh, echoed from the kitchen.

"Mom? Is that you?"

"In here, dear," she said, though America couldn't think of a good reason that her mother was in her apartment and not gallivanting through grapevines in Italy.

Turning the corner, her mother and father stood at the island, canoodling, and making a giant mess of America's kitchenware. With arms out wide, she embraced her parents together and squeezed them tightly. They smelled different than she remembered, like all the tomatoes and olive oil they had enjoyed whilst overseas had seeped through their pores.

"I don't understand. What are you doing here?" America looked at her parents in turn, and held her father's hand on her right and her mother's hand in the other. "You have another few days left in Italy."

"I got your message," her mom said. "And we got on the first flight."

"Not the first one," her dad added. "We tried to call you back. And I know you warned us that the reception wasn't great in Christmas Cove. Your mother called your assistant, Poppy?"

America nodded and threw her palm against her own forehead. "What did she tell you?"

"About the boy, you mean?" her mom nudged.

"And?"

"Is it true? You fell for the mayor?" her dad asked.

174

Was it true that everyone around her seemed to know she was in love with Leo, and she was the only person in denial? She had only known him for a few days. It was impossible to love someone so fast. Her revelation with Mark back at the office had opened her eyes. Being infatuated with someone fogs the view. *Fog*, she thought of standing at the top of the bluff with Leo and looking down on the empty plain with fog crowding in from the south that first morning.

"Leo, the mayor, was a very nice man," she said.

"He *was* nice, but isn't anymore?" her dad asked.

"Is. Was. It doesn't matter because I ruined everything," America said and walked to the living room and directly towards the tree. "I was selfish, and rude, and bossy, and . . ." She stopped herself from that line of toxic thoughts. "Needless to say, the week was a total waste of time, and I should have just stayed in my lane." America turned to her mother, who had followed her out of the kitchen. "This is what makes me a good editor, defined parameters."

Her mom placed her hands on America's shoulders and straightened them. "You like him that much?"

A nod was all she could muster past the tears that welled in her eyes. "I'm scared," America admitted.

"Oh, dear." Her mom pulled her in close. "I've not seen you like this before. You've got it bad."

"I've never felt like this, and I'm so uncertain as to what I should do about it. I wish I could just forget the whole thing."

"That, unfortunately, is not how life works. Some things you just can't come back from. So, how can we help? You mentioned the city was in some legal trouble?" her mom said.

America's father emerged from the kitchen with a small charcuterie board of cheese, bread, and olive oil, and she realized that she had been smelling the food when she first came home, and not her parents permeated by the scents of

Italy. A smile pulled up on one side of her face, and she took a chunk of French bread.

"Let me start at the beginning." America took a second to straighten out her thoughts while she swirled the bread in the spiced oil. "A few years ago, a nor'easter hit the area and blew out the dam, which was the main reason people lived there around the lake. People began moving away and now there aren't enough residents to support the city's basic obligations. The neighboring town, Elizabethtown, will incorporate the Cove if they don't have a hundred-fifty residents by Christmas Eve."

"This is why the magazine sent you there? Seems like an odd thing to cover," her mom said.

"Not exactly. The mayor called and set this up with the magazine to cover the idyllic Christmas celebrations." America thought about Leo's possible reasons for wanting the magazine to do an article in the first place. "Now that I think about it, it doesn't make any sense at all."

"What part?" her dad asked.

"Why would Leo have asked for the magazine to feature the city's holiday events when there wasn't any planned? It was almost as though the town wasn't expecting to see me, or anyone else from a travel magazine, at all this year."

"How do you mean?"

"Think about it. If you invited a writer to your town, wouldn't you have wanted to put your best foot, or in this case, holiday show, forward?" America said and paced in front of the tree.

"I see what you mean," her mother said and took a bite of bread dipped in the oil. When she was finished chewing, she added, "So, either the mayor set you up to embarrass the town, or he really knew nothing about it."

America remembered the look on Leo's face as she accused him of doing nothing and not caring what happened to the Cove. It was not the look of a man who had been found out. It was the look of a man who had just been stabbed in the heart.

America covered her mouth with the back of her hand. "I made a huge mistake," she whispered. "The last thing I said to him was that he didn't care about the town, or the people, and he was crushed. I had no right to say anything to him about anything."

America whipped out her phone and opened a text to Poppy.

> FIND OUT WHO REQUESTED THE FEATURE ON CHRISTMAS COVE ASAP.

"Dad, is there anything legally that will help the Cove?"

"I don't know, hon. I have to look up the statutes and—how many people do they need to move in?"

"It was six, but Jenny Townsend had her baby early. So," America said, thinking about the tiny baby who didn't even know they were helping to save Christmas.

"Well, we got three, right here. So that leaves two more to go," Mom said, and America spit out the cheese she had just begun to chew.

"Excuse me! What? I never said I was moving to Christmas Cove." The idea was preposterous, though Leo had suggested the same thing in jest. The question swirled: Why couldn't she? What was keeping her in the city? She could do her job from anywhere, and she would certainly like to work in a more secluded setting than the one her glass pen provided.

"For as long as I've known you, you have loved everything about Christmas, from the decorations to the giving, to the smiles and twinkling lights, and the merriment you can bring to the community around you. I, for one, can't imagine you living out your days anywhere else than somewhere named for the holiday. Plus," her mom put her hand on her dad's knee the way America had touched Leo in the truck to reassure him, "your father and I are tired of the city and thinking about making a big change."

"How so?" America said slowly as though she was afraid of what her parents would say next.

"Now that your father has retired, I have decided to finally follow my dream of opening my own boutique," her mom said.

America couldn't believe it. Her mom had spoken about her idea for a little shop that would carry local artisan crafts and apparel and furniture for years. "That's wonderful! But, if not in the city, then where?"

Mom looked at Dad and they both cracked a mirrored smiled. "Christmas Cove." They said in unison.

"What do you think?" her mom asked. "In one of the photos you sent of Main Street, I believe I noticed a For Sale sign in one of the windows, and well . . ."

"We missed you very much while we were away in Italy. If you go, we go too," Dad finished.

America's phone buzzed with a message from Poppy.

ON IT. STAND BY

America tapped the corner of the phone into her open palm. If Leo hadn't requested the article, then who?

"I'm a little on edge," America said and sat across from her parents. "Distract me, will you? How was your trip? Other than shortened."

"We had a wonderful time. I got to see where Papoosh grew up in a village at the base of the Alps. It was out of a storybook. Ripped from a different time. I have a ton of pictures."

Her mom motioned for America to come and sit beside

her. She swiped through photos of picturesque country sides filled with grapevines and dotted with tiny villages. There were photos of narrow, sun-drenched streets lined with towering cypress trees, and bustling holiday markets overflowing with handcrafted trinkets and delicious foods.

"This looks incredible. I might have to go someday myself. So, why didn't you want to stay?" America said and shut off the screen. "I'm a big girl, you know. I could have handled this on my own."

"We know," her dad said. "Honestly, although it was a beautiful place, we were tired of all the commotion, and when we got your message, it was just the excuse we needed to head home a little sooner than planned."

"Thanks, Dad. It actually means a lot to me that you're here."

America's phone buzzed again. "It's Poppy," she said to no one in particular, but didn't want her parents to think she was being rude.

> MAYOR THORPE. OF ELIZABETHTOWN.
> CALL SOON

America read the text aloud.

"What does that mean?" her mom asked.

"It means that it wasn't Leo at all. The whole time, I had assumed he was the person who had requested the feature. I even asked him about it on a couple of occasions, but I think I got distracted or something, because I kind of dropped it."

"Why would the other mayor do that?" America's mom asked while her dad got up and paced. His deep breaths and distant eyes meant he was working the problem.

"Maybe this Mayor Thorpe hoped to embarrass Leo and gain some support for when the incorporation goes through. He'd look like a hero, coming in and saving it all," her dad said.

"That may have been his plan, but I didn't write that article about how sad the town was without its Christmas. Instead, I sprinkled lights and ornaments around the town and made believe it was back. Heck, I even went to Elizabethtown and handed out fliers declaring as much." America joined her dad's pacing.

"You also may have saved the town," her dad chimed in and was already scrolling on his phone. "This mayor of Elizabethtown might have broken the law, and the incorporation might be at risk of falling through. This might take some time, but I have a few ideas."

While her dad got to work making calls in the other room, America sat beside her mother. "What do I do?"

"Let me ask you something. Even if the town is taken over, can't there still be the neighborhood of Christmas Cove, and can't there still be holiday traditions? When we drove through some of the tiny little villages in Italy, there were plenty that had less than a hundred people living there. But each had their own unique feeling and personality. Can't this be the same, whether it's its own town or not?"

America hadn't thought about it that way. Just as the different areas of any big city have their distinct cultures, why couldn't that be true for the Cove also? And if that was ultimately the outcome, what should the city name on the postbox matter to her, or Leo, or Carol, or Edwin, or anyone else for that matter?

"There's only one thing you're forgetting. I insulted Leo's character in the most dishonorable way. I don't think he'll forgive me."

"Will you fight for him?" her mom asked.

America hesitated and stared at the tree, remembering the cross ornament she had taken with her to the cabin. The ornament that she had left behind in her haste to depart. The ornament hanging on the tree that Leo had brought her. Leo.

She turned and nodded to her mother. "I forgot something very dear to me there. I'm going back. Are you sure you both want to come with me?"

"I wouldn't miss this for the world," her dad chimed in from the kitchen.

"Pack it up?" her mom said with a smile from ear to ear. The twinkling lights reflected in her happy eyes.

"I have to do something first," America said and grabbed her bag off the hook by the front door. "We can leave tomorrow."

# CHAPTER 29

WITH NOTHING LEFT TO KICK, LEO RESORTED TO THROWING the sheets and blankets from the cabin bed into a pile in the corner. "How could she just leave like this?"

"You want a real answer, or do you want me to throw a fit with you?" Edwin said.

Edwin was right, throwing a fit would not bring America back. He had been so stupid to drive away that evening, the way he had. His wounded pride was no good excuse for the way he had behaved. Since his parents had passed away, he had done everything he could to sabotage his chance at happiness, thinking he didn't deserve what they had. And now, his one real shot was long gone.

He flopped onto the stripped mattress and squeezed his eyes shut. "I'm the stupidest person that ever lived," he whined.

"So, now it's a pity party, and not a fit," Edwin said. "I suppose I'll have to join you."

"What do you have to be pitiful about?" Leo lay down and stared at the ceiling.

"I liked that city girl. And I'm gonna miss her being around town and causing me more work."

Leo had to laugh at that. "Pa, you sound sadder than me. What are we going to do about all this?"

"You know, it was my suggestion that you keep her in town in the first place. You can take it out on me if that will help."

Taking his frustration out on something seemed like a solid idea, but Edwin was not that thing. Leo had only himself to blame for the predicament he was drowning in. America had hit a nerve when she had called him out for not doing enough for the town. But it wasn't due to his lack of caring. He loved the place so much and wanted nothing more than to preserve it as it had been in his youth.

She was right about one thing. He could have done more. Progress of any kind seemed antithetical to his ends, and he had spent most of his time as mayor avoiding acting on any innovative ideas. It wasn't until America swept into town that he started thinking about new possibilities. After the dam broke and the lake emptied, he planted his feet in the concrete. But the cement had turned to quicksand, and he was slowly sinking, along with the whole town, past the point of no return.

"I need to get her back, Pa. She was the brightest ray of sunshine I've seen in longer than I care to admit," Leo said and walked to the living area. He looked at the little tree, with its one strand of lights and its smattering of ornaments, and imagined a life where he and America could conquer Christmas together each year. "I need to make some things right, and then I can grovel properly."

"Anything I can help with?" Edwin asked. "You want me to take this tree down?"

"No," Leo said and held a silver cross in his fingers, not one of the ornaments that he had brought over. "Leave it up for now. I'm heading over to the Townsends' to see that little baby of theirs."

AT THE RANCH ON THE EDGE OF TOWN, LEO GRABBED THE TRAY of lasagna he had prepared earlier in the day. He didn't know much about infants, but he was sure the last thing that his friend Cam or Jenny wanted to do was cook food.

"Hey, brother," Cam said and met him at the door. "I'm glad to see you." He took the glass tray. "And I'm glad to see you brought food."

"It was no problem," Leo said and followed Cam inside.

Cam's face was a mix of exhaustion and elation, but Leo could see how the tiny new addition to their family had already filled the home with joy.

"Come in and take a seat. Jenny is resting upstairs. As you can imagine, having a baby is a lot of work. Can I get you a beer?"

Leo checked the time. It was early, but he figured why not? "What do you have?"

"Same old," Cam said.

"You need to try Pa's new brew. It's surprisingly good. Not that his other attempts have been bad, just boring. But the one I had last week was refreshing and tasted like home."

Cam laughed. "So, he's roped you into his hobby, too? That old man has more energy than our four-day-old baby at feeding time."

Leo took a long swig from the longneck and let the cool liquid rush down his throat. It had been an unexpectedly challenging time over the last week. Though he had loved every moment he had spent with America Greene, he needed a break from the regrets clouding his mind.

"Speaking of feedings," Cam said. "The little one is gonna be up soon. She's been down for about an hour already."

"Should I have called before dropping by?" Leo asked.

"Nah. Babies sleep when they want and wake when they want. You can't really get a schedule going at first. No, I'm glad you stopped by."

"What name did you decide on?" Leo asked.

"Charlotte Victoria," Cam beamed.

"That's beautiful."

"Thanks. It was Jenny's idea to have such an important sounding name. My family goes all the way back to the founding of this nation, and she felt it was right to honor that legacy."

"I love that. You two are going to be such great parents."

"And what about you? Any family in your future?"

"That was to the point," Leo said and shifted his weight in the leather recliner. "Is everyone talking about it?"

"Everyone and their dog," Cam laughed. "Are you going to marry this woman from the city?"

Marry her? Leo had only just met her. How could he want to, or know whether she was the one? "I don't know, man. It's a little fast."

Cam shrugged. "Jenny would have said yes on our first date. At least I like to think that's how good my charms are."

"You did get serious pretty quick."

"What can I say? When you know, you know." Cam chuckled. "So, what's the problem?"

"I was an ass. And she went home after accusing me of not doing enough as mayor." Leo took another drink. "The worst of it, she was right."

"Did you ask her to stay?"

"Wouldn't that have been the simplest thing to do?" Leo downed the rest of the beer before it warmed up from the heat of his hand around the glass bottle and took the moment to consider Cam's question.

"You love her, huh?" Cam said. "Man, I knew it the

moment you pulled into my driveway with that sick, sad, puppy-dog look on your face. But don't worry. I got you covered."

"What do you mean?" Leo said, his interest piqued.

Cam left the room, and Leo heard the back door swing open and shut with a thud. Leo stood and walked off his nerves at whatever his friend was up to. The fireplace crackled in front of him and caused him to replay the night of the bonfire in his mind. He had wanted to kiss America so badly and mourned not doing so. He could taste her sweetness on his lips but had pulled away before allowing himself the indulgence.

His reverie was interrupted by the sound of the back door creaking open and slamming shut again.

Cam returned with a small wood box, about six inches square, in his hand. "This is just the thing you need."

Leo opened the lid and gave a half-cocked grin. "When did you—how?" Leo stammered at the glittering sight.

"I had a feeling, about a week ago," Cam shut the lid. "Wasn't even sure who I was making this piece for. And now I know."

"This ring is perfect." Leo ran his finger over the edges of the cut stones mounted on a silvery band. "You're a true artist, Cameron Townsend. I owe you one. Or ten thousand," Leo said and palmed the box. "Thank you. And tell Jenny hello for me."

"I will, and thanks for bringing us dinner," Cam said as the two shook hands. "But don't think a meal alone is payment enough for what's in that box."

"Send me a bill," Leo said and got out of there.

# CHAPTER 30

AMERICA'S "TOMORROW" HAD TURNED INTO FIVE LONG DAYS. She had lost count of how many phone calls and emails she had exchanged between her and the realtor, and between her and the bank. Purchasing a home was a far different exercise in patience than scooping up an apartment in the city. Her mind swam laps between the things she had been busy doing in preparation for her return to the Cove, and the things she planned to do whenever she finally got back there.

With all the groundwork laid, she shot off a quick note to Mr. Janowitz asking him to hold the article for as long as possible. The story wasn't finished yet, and she had somewhere to be.

Finally on the road, she set the cruise control of her dad's SUV to six miles above the posted speed limit. Though she felt uncomfortable about breaking the rules, time was not on her side. She had spent several more days in the city than she had wanted to, but what she was planning to surprise Leo with had to be done right. She used her time traveling the winding road northward to calculate the precise amount of apologizing and groveling that would be necessary to convey her sincere regret at how she had treated Leo. The only thing standing in her way was a long-awaited cold front bearing down on the northeast.

"Are you sure you don't want your father to drive?" her mom asked from the back seat.

"And risk him falling asleep at the wheel? I'd rather not."

America's father lifted his head from the side window where he rested it, already half asleep. "I'm not tired," he said.

"I can't believe how jet-lagged you both still are," America said.

"They say it's harder to go west. I think that's right," her mom said. "Either way. We're old, and old people get tired and stay tired."

"You're not even that old."

"Fifty-nine this year," her dad said.

"That makes one of us. You hit that milestone years ago, dear," her mom shot back.

America loved her parents' senses of humor and wanted that kind of playful affection for herself someday. She and Leo had bantered so naturally with each other, she wondered if that sort of ease was such a rare thing to find.

"Why don't you two nod off for a bit while I drive? I have some thinking to do," America suggested and got no complaints from the gallery.

"Sounds good to me." America's dad pulled his coat around his chest and laid his head back against the side window.

The drive started out with fair weather, but an hour north of the city, the sunny skies gave way to clouds. A light drizzle began to mist the windshield and crystalize at the edges. With the cold front coming across, and darkness quickly approaching, America took the drive with more caution. Once the GPS told her to exit the highway, she knew the roads would narrow and snake tightly around the countryside. From valleys to hilltops and everything in between, road conditions were likely to deteriorate.

The sun dipped below the cloud bank to the southwest and caused the gray branches and weathered fences to glow gold, before disappearing completely beneath the horizon. Her smile switched to a tense focus, and she squinted as she looked into the dusk ahead.

As soon as the sun went down, she knew she was in trouble. Within minutes, the damp roads had frozen in the areas that received little to no warmth throughout the day. Icy roads weren't something she ever had to contend with in the city.

Her tires ran between wet patches and icy slicks. The car didn't seem to know what to do with the lack of traction, and neither did America. It wasn't until the wheels spun one direction, and the car traveled in the opposite direction that she realized how wholly unequipped for country life she truly was. She turned the steering wheel in the direction that the car was going like she had witnessed someone do in a movie once.

The jostling stirred her parents. "Watch out!" her dad said.

America tried to do what she could, but the car had a destination of its own, right into the gravel shoulder. Regaining a sliver of control, she slammed her foot on the brakes and put the gear into park.

Her dad's hand fell on her knee. "It's ok. We're all right."

"It was just a patch of ice. Once I hit it, there was nothing I could do. But I need a minute." America grabbed her coat from the backseat and got out of the car.

Running off the road had her shaking, or perhaps it was the cold that had arrived as though on cue to ruin her chance of getting to Leo before it was too late. She rolled her sleeve back and checked the time. Two days, and the fate of

Christmas Cove would be sealed one way or another. Behind her, her mother tapped on the window and rolled it halfway down.

"Whoa! It's freezing out there. I guess you're getting your winter after all," Mom said. "You ready to get back in and get going? The roads aren't getting any less icy with all this drizzle, and your father says we're nearly there. He'll drive if you want."

America nodded to both questions, though she seriously considered walking the rest of the way. If it weren't for the freezing rain and fog encapsulating her in winter's prison, and her lack of arctic hiking gear at that moment, she might have taken to walking across the empty fields to get to the cabin.

She walked to the passenger side, passing her father on the way around. She opened the passenger side door, and the glass reflected oncoming headlights into her eyes. The vehicle slowed as it approached her location, but she was unable to see beyond the blinding lights. The vehicle swerved on the road and came to a stop facing America head on, the way one would do if having to jump a car battery.

"Everything all right over there?" a voice called out from the driver's side window.

America's dad waved. "Hit a bit of ice, but we're just getting on our way now. Thanks, neighbor."

America's ears had already pricked up. The voice was too much like Leo's smooth baritone to be anyone else. She was half inside the passenger side door when he called out to her.

"America? Is that you?"

Flipping up the hood of her coat, she stepped carefully over the slick gravel towards him. As her pace increased, so did the pounding in her chest and the flutter returned to her belly.

He matched her speed with deliberate steps. His breath, ragged and visible in the cold. "What are you doing here?"

America looked around—for what exactly, she wasn't certain. A way out perhaps? "How did you know where to find us?"

Leo looked around her towards the SUV with a brow raised as if he was wondering who she was with but didn't want to ask. He took another step closer.

"My parents are with me." She pointed and looked over her shoulder, where her parents were waving out of the windows. She bit her lips and squashed a giggle as she turned back to Leo, who had taken one more step towards her. He was dangerously close. If she wanted, she could reach out and touch him. She could wrap her arms around his neck and say all the things she had practiced in her mind during the drive. Instead, America buried her hands in her pockets. "How did you find me?"

"I was on my way to the cabin to meet with a new guest when I saw the swerving headlights. I didn't know it was you."

"Would that have changed your mind about coming to my aid?" America's heart hammered against her ribs, and she was glad her puffy coat was big enough to hide her nerves.

"America, of course I would help you. Just as I would help anyone in need. I would hope that was clear about me."

She could hear the hurt in his voice. The wound that she had caused with her accusations of him not caring about the people in Christmas Cove was still open and oozing.

"Why are you here, America?"

"I came back to see you. To apologize . . ." She blinked away a cold tear. "For so many things."

Leo kicked the gravel and shrugged. "I don't know whether I should be pleased to see you or irritated that you think you can just roll up to town and make everything OK."

"I have a whole speech prepared," she said and closed the space between them. "I didn't know what I was talking about that last time we spent together. Everything seemed too good, and I assumed the worst about you."

Leo stood only inches away now and his heat radiated off of him. Her belly tightened and her cheeks warmed at the proximity. She wanted to kiss him, to feel his strong, supple lips against hers, and to close her eyes and forget the wintry world around her.

"I'm sorry," she whispered, and he leaned in.

Leo's eyes closed, and the air stilled around them. He breathed in through his nose and hesitated for a moment. Energy scattered like a million pieces of confetti in her chest in the tense silence. She licked her lips.

Leo backed away. "Do you need help getting back on the road?" His voice was calm and steady as though he had switched gears into mayor mode.

"No." America took a step backwards. The car's head-lights lit the fog around her and Leo. She could clearly see his face and knew by the neutral smile that their conversation was over. For the moment. "My dad is going to drive. Thanks for checking on this situation."

"Where are you staying?" he asked.

"I have a reservation at a local place," she said. "It's booked under my mom's name, Vivian Rosa."

"Of course, it would be the cabin." Leo turned back to his truck and reached in through the driver's window. He held out a set of keys and jingled them as he walked back to her. "Here. You know where the cabin is. Fully stocked and ready to go."

Removing one hand from her pocket, she took the keys. Her fingers brushed against his and their gaze met like two ships in the night. He might be mad at her, but there was no doubt after that subtle touch that something was still brewing between them.

"Thank you, Leo."

"Let me know if you need anything, and enjoy your stay in Christmas Cove." Leo's formality stung her.

"Can we get going?" America's dad yelled out.

America locked her eyes on Leo's truck as he pulled out and drove past her. The realization hit her mind that, like the ice pellets hitting her face, winning the man over was going to be harder than she had hoped.

# CHAPTER 31

AMERICA WASTED NO TIME IN THE MORNING. HER PARENTS were still asleep as she crawled out of the loft and climbed down the ladder. Grabbing a pen and paper from the drawer beside the fridge, she wrote a note letting them know she was heading into town. Although, there was no need to worry about them. They had just spent a week traipsing across northern Italy, they could certainly handle themselves in Christmas Cove.

She reached for a granola bar from a basket on the kitchen island and shoved it in her coat pocket. Winter emanated from the windows, having arrived via the cold front overnight, and she would have started the fireplace if she were staying in. Outside the cabin, there was no snow on the ground, but with temperatures as cold as they were, she hoped it wouldn't be long before the white stuff would flock the town. In the meantime, she wrapped her scarf around her neck and made her way out to the front porch.

"Morning sunshine."

America screamed as she flung around. "Dad? You frightened me. I thought you were still asleep."

He sat, rocking in a wooden chair on the porch. A plaid blanket draped across his legs, and he held a mug of something that was no longer steaming in his right hand. He looked at peace with a brightness in his eyes.

The sun was coming up and would soon be above the clouds. She knew from experience that the fog would roll in soon thereafter, and the day would turn to the bleak gray she had become accustomed to. It dawned on her, if she stayed in Christmas Cove, it was a view she would be living with for some time to come.

"Where are you running off to?" Dad asked.

"Main Street. I have a meeting with one of the town elders, Carol. She's great. You'll like her. She's sort of salty though, until you get to know her." America pulled on her gloves and made certain her laces were tight on her boots. "Any luck on the legal front?"

"Actually, I did hear back from my colleague that works in municipal law. He says the statute is clear, and both cities ratified it a hundred years ago. I doubt either town ever saw anything like this happening, but the idea is honorable. It provides that if one city should fall below the threshold that the other city will support its financial and governmental obligations."

"So, there's no way to break it?" she asked.

"Do you even want to?"

"I don't know. It seems unfair to the people that are still here. This is their town. But what you're saying is that the two towns had an agreement to help each other, either way the chips fell?"

"You got it," her dad said. "I don't know what's right for this place, but the law is the law. If the people here are determined to save the town, their best chance is to find those last couple of people to move here. Your mom is excited about her new venture here, and well, I'm a retired man now, and," he continued the next part with a British accent, "I'm at my leisure." He sipped his coffee. "Cold," he said. "I'm going to pour a fresh cup."

Her dad rose from the rocking chair and placed the blanket over the seat back as though he had done the action a million times. The country suited him, and America could already see a change, a sort of calmness, wash over him. She embraced him with one arm and let him pass.

"Wait." America flipped around. "I forgot to ask you. Didn't you say you thought the other mayor—Mayor Thorpe —may have broken the law? Do you have anything new about that?"

"It doesn't seem like there was a personal or financial conflict. All he did was request the article feature from your magazine. And since it wasn't even about his own town, there is nothing he did wrong. In fact, if your plan works out for Christmas Cove, then his actions might constitute an in-kind donation to Leo here. And that's a whole other situation."

America considered the information and the question he posed a moment earlier. Would it really be the worst thing for Elizabethtown to help support the area? In the reverse situation, she knew that the people in Christmas Cove would gladly help their neighbors, too. "Thanks for checking on it anyway."

"It was no trouble, really," her dad said and gave her a quick hug. "Did anything come of the plea your assistant put in the teaser for the article?" he asked at the door.

America nodded. "I don't know. Anyway, we only have two days, and I doubt people will be clamoring to move here." Checking her watch, she said, "I have to go. I'll catch up with you and Mom later."

. . .

THE WALK TO TOWN WAS SHORT. THE GRAVEL ROAD WAS AS familiar to her now as though she'd lived there her whole life. It was a feeling, one of comfort, that she had experienced on multiple occasions since first arriving in town. Despite its initial lack of holly berries and glitter, she was fond of the place in a way she had never felt for the city she called home.

Before deciding to move the Cove, Mr. Janowitz had reassured her that she could work remotely, and that she only would need to come into the office a few times a year. Though, if her plan were going to work, she would require a more reliable internet connection than the one that the town currently offered.

America checked the time, though it didn't matter anymore. There was both too little time, and all the time in the world now. The article would tell the truth about the Cove. The only way for readers to understand how special Christmas Cove is, is to show it through the eyes of the people who called it home. She included stories from Pa and Carol, things she had learned about while researching at the library, and some calls she'd made to other residents over the past few days.

One thing she was certain of, Christmas Cove wasn't going anywhere, no matter what happened to the postal code or city name. Now that she had bought a house in town, she would stay and make things right with Leo, however long it took.

At Carol's door, America knocked softly at first, and then rang the bell. Nerves coursed through her, and she tapped her foot on the threshold step, though she blamed her fidgeting on the cold and not on the tension in her muscles. The door opened and a bright-eyed, silver-haired Carol smiled out of the crack.

"America! Come in. Come in. You must be freezing out there." She closed the door and unlatched the chain before opening the door all the way. "Leo said you had gone back to the big city."

"I did, but did he tell you why?"

Carol took America's coat and hung it over a kitchen chair. "He said you had work to get back to. He seemed sad. Maybe upset? Did you get into a tiff?"

"Carol, I've royally screwed this one up."

America recounted the entire story. She told Carol that she had accused Leo of not even caring about the town, and how he had trusted her only for her to throw it back at him and break that trust.

"And now, I've learned that Elizabethtown's mayor, was the one who requested the article, my article, about Christmas Cove, and not Leo who I had assumed was the person that originally contacted the magazine. I can't know for sure what his angle was, but I doubt he wanted someone sweeping in here and bringing back Christmas like I did."

"Could it be that he doesn't want to take over our town at all? Perhaps this is exactly what he wanted." Carol said and tapped her fingers against her lips as she pondered. "Doesn't seem right though, does it?"

"Not at all. I imagine he wants the Cove for some benefit. I just don't know what it is yet," America said. She had gone over and over in her head about the mayor's possible reasons. Money was likely involved somehow, but until she could dig more into the politics and scheming, the mystery would remain. "We may never know that man's real reasons behind the article request. Although, I intend to find out. My suspicion is that he was hoping to embarrass the Cove and have a grand reopening of sorts under a new city banner, but that's a stretch without more evidence."

"I tend to agree with you," Carol said. "But what can we do about it?"

"We need the people. Plain as that." America took the

woman's hands in hers. "I really am sorry. I just wanted to help the Cove reclaim some of its Christmas cheer. Things got out of hand so fast."

"You know, America. Christmas Cove is just a place—"

"I had thought that earlier, on my way back to town."

"No, I don't think you understand." Carol poured a cup of coffee, even though America didn't ask for one and Carol hadn't inquired. "Christmas is something that lives in your heart. It's a feeling. It's knowing that you are loved—"

"It's all this!" America pointed to the coffee in a red mug, and to the kitchen around them with a small Christmas tree tucked into one corner and holly berry placemats on the table.

Carol nodded. "You got so caught up in wanting to fix everything that you forgot to look around at what really needs fixing. This town, whether it is or isn't one going forward, has been a place that generations of people remember for our Christmas spirit and summertime musings. They won't love it less if it's part of Elizabethtown, you know."

America blew on the coffee and slurped. "Thank you. Not just for the coffee, but for the perspective. You've given me much to think about."

"Now," Carol beamed and slapped her own knee. "What are we going to do about you and Leo? I've never seen him look at anyone the way he looked at you at the Christmas tree lighting. There's something there. I just know it. That man has never so much as hinted at finding love, and then, BAM! You show up and he's a pool of joy and distress. I doubt he saw it coming any more than you did."

Carol's insight was frighteningly accurate. America had not been looking for love, but had found something she suspected could be the real thing. "Distress? If you mean that he's confused about pursuing a relationship with someone he just met, and who turned his entire world upside down, then I know what you mean."

"What's your plan?" Carol asked, grinning. "You must have something in mind, since you came back here."

What was she going to do? America had a wake of first dates behind her that she was certain hadn't led to a second date because of her. No matter how good her intentions were, she knew now that she had gotten in her own way in all of her previous relationships. The truth was made clear back at the office when swoon-worthy Mark had ceased to thrill her in any measurable way.

It wasn't infatuation, or an impressive resume, which had attracted her to Leo. From the beginning, she had fallen for his kindness and the way they laughed together. She wasn't sure what love would feel like, but the fluttering in her belly, the way her pulse quickened whenever he looked at her, and the way she wanted to move mountains, or in this case move copious amounts of Christmas decorations, for him and with him, told her this was something different. Something special.

"I see you're thinking about him," Carol interrupted. "You should tell him."

"How do you mean?" America said. "Was I thinking aloud? I do that sometimes."

"No. But I know that look on your face. The one that says you're calculating your feelings and it's scary." Carol brought her cup to the sink and turned on the water. She began washing her mug while she spoke. "I know that look well. I wore it once when I was a little younger than you are now. You'll regret it forever if you don't act on it."

America wondered if Carol's memory had something to do with the story that Edwin had told her about their date at the winter formal. "Do you still regret it?" she asked without adding specifics to the question.

"Edwin told you?" Carol turned off the water and dried the mug with a red and green plaid dish towel.

America nodded. "You wish things would have gone differently?"

"I wish I would have at least told him about my father's temper. But you know, time passed, and we never spoke of it again. Seems odd that he would bring it up after all these years."

"It's my fault. I was curious and asked why they call you Scrooge," America admitted. "I was nosy, and I'm sorry."

"Don't be." Carol laughed it off. "You live in a small place like this, and soon enough, everyone knows everything about everybody. Heck! You're the first new thing we've had to talk about in years."

"I'm glad I could serve some purpose, then." America laughed.

"One thing everyone is going to ask is, why did you come back here? Just for Leo?"

America stood and walked to the front room. Pulling back the edge of the red sheer drapes, she pointed to the row of buildings across the street. "See that one, there? The Victorian one with pink trim?"

Carol craned her neck, as the building was slightly down the street from her own house. "The old Manner Manor?"

America giggled just as she had when the realtor had told her the name of the home three days earlier. "I bought it. It needs some renovations, you know."

"You mean . . . we're going to be neighbors?"

This revelation had already put a pep in Carol's step, and she seemed to be standing straighter than before. America smiled and nodded her head.

"But, why? For Leo?" Carol asked.

"I can't lie and say he had nothing to do with my decision, but it's more than that. I've fallen in love with this tiny town, and as strange as it sounds, I know somehow that I'm a part of its future."

"I think so too." Carol took America's hands in hers. "And wait, that means we only need four more residents. I heard a rumor about some family wanting to move in."

"My parents are also moving here. That means we only need two more." America announced. "After I got them up to speed, they didn't hesitate to come with me. They really are the best parents. You're gonna love them."

"I can't wait to meet them. Where are they now?" Carol asked.

"Here. At the cabin."

Carol clapped her hands in excitement. "What a merry Christmas!"

"I hope so," America said. "Now, about Leo."

"Just tell him how you feel, and everything will work out. Have some faith."

"Then wish me luck," America said and put her coat back on. "Feels like snow out there."

"Feels like magic in the air." Carol smiled and gave an exaggerated wink as she shoved America into the cold.

# CHAPTER 32

As soon as America's feet hit the crest of the dirt road, she stopped walking. The fog had stayed away for now, and the view of the countryside was spectacular from the vantage point. So was the view of Leo's red truck parked at the bottom of the drive, in front of the cabin. She fidgeted with the coat's fit and smoothed the front as though she were donning armor. The next encounter with Leo could go one of two ways in her estimation: either unbelievably bad, or not that bad. No matter the outcome, the conversation would start with honesty.

With the attitude of a sailor walking the plank, she headed for the inevitable. Her steps quickened, and she soon found herself at a full gallop towards destiny. Stomping up the front steps, she slowed and took a deep breath before letting herself through the front door. Her eyes scanned the living room and kitchen in fast repetition but only spotted her mom sitting on the sofa, and her dad with his head buried in the fridge.

"You're back," Dad said as he peeked above the fridge door.

Still out of breath and regretting having run, America said, "Truck. Leo." She pointed and hoped her parents would know what she wanted.

"Oh. That. Yes. Leo, the mayor, was just here. Nice fellow," her father said.

America's mother came to the kitchen and sat at the counter. "I like him a lot. Genuinely nice to look at, too."

"Mom!" America scolded. "What did he want?"

"Now, don't be mad . . ."

That warning alone was enough to make America's heart rate skyrocket. "What did you do?"

"Nothing. Just . . . I called him and asked him to come over," her mom said.

"Why would you do that?" America paced in front of the door.

"Because I knew you wouldn't. And we wanted to meet him properly."

"Please tell me you didn't embarrass me." America shuddered to think what her parents could have said to the man.

"Of course not. But we told him that you needed to speak with him," Dad said.

"Where is he now?" America scanned the space.

"He said you would know where to find him."

America suspected. "What if I'd been gone for hours? He was just going to wait all day?"

"I don't know. I'm not a miracle worker," her dad said and cracked open a bottle of red wine. She looked at him questioningly and pointed at her watch face. He shrugged. "What? I like wine with lunch now. Anyway, the point is, he's here, somewhere, and so are you. All you need to do is talk to him before he finds out from someone else that you're moving here."

America bundled up again and walked to the door as if her feet were making the decisions for her now.

Her mother added, "Tell him how you really feel, and the rest will work out."

It was the second time she had heard that same advice in the last hour. Perhaps it was a God-wink, or simply sage wisdom from people that had lived a bit more life than she had so far. With a heart full of sense, she headed for the gravel path that led down to the dock.

The closer she came to the old dock, the more fog rolled in. The midday sun scattered pockets of light through the fog, and visibility shifted from about twenty feet to near zero at random intervals. Having spent time there already, America had learned to take steps along the path with confidence, as the material was unforgiving with its slick and movable surface. Even so, she walked as fast as felt safe.

The path gave way to the gray boards and splintered handrail of the defunct dock where she fully expected to see Leo come into sight. But the dock was empty. She walked all the way to the end and shouted his name into the empty cove. The sound echoed in the abyss, and she hollered again.

America looked over the rail on both sides and searched the visible shoreline. Illuminated by a pocket of sunlight, the silhouette of a man appeared on the old, pebbled shore. A charred crater surrounded by a circle of larger stones lay to his right. It was where they had shared an evening beside a roaring bonfire.

She hurried off the dock and ran towards him. "Leo," she shouted. "I'm coming."

Leo turned around, lit by a sliver of sunlight, a half grin pulled at one side of his face, but he remained in place where he stood. Unlike the previous night when they met on the icy roadside by chance, he had moved towards her, seriously close to her.

"My parents told me you were waiting for me," America said as she approached.

"They said you needed to talk."

She slowed and put her hands out to him. He took her hands, and they stood face to face. He didn't look mad, just really tired. His eyes tilted down at the sides and his lips were thin and chalky.

"Where to start," she mumbled and looked down at her feet to make certain they hadn't gotten an idea to escape. With feet planted on firm ground, she steeled her nerve. *The truth.* "I need to apologize to you. Really apologize. That's why I'm here."

"That's not necessary, America—"

"It is. Now let me finish." She waited for him to nod, and he threw in a soft grin. "That night we were here. I promised you something that I had no right to do."

"About keeping the Christmas traditions alive? That was harmless," he said.

"No. Well, yes, I did say that. But I'm talking about the promise I made with my heart. You opened up to me and trusted me. I broke that trust, and the promise of what we were building together, and for that, I'm sorry."

"You think we were building something?" he asked and pulled her hands a little closer. His eyes turned up at the sides a little.

"Yes?" she said without hesitation.

"And what were we building, exactly?"

She could tell he wanted to hear the words. He wanted her to confide in him, the way he had confided in her. "I like you, Leo. A lot. And I think you like me too." America's words fell out like a waterfall, and were more scattered than she liked, but continued despite the mess. "I never planned on any of this. I came here to write a story for the magazine. The mayor had requested a feature on the Christmas traditions of the Cove, of which there were none when I arrived."

"That's what you kept getting at with your questions. No

wonder you were confused." He shook his head in disbelief as he spoke. "I never requested a feature," he said.

"No, you didn't. But I didn't know that at the time. Besides, I needed something to write about. So, I decided to bring back Christmas, whether the town wanted it or not. When I found out you were the mayor, I figured you had been the one to ask the magazine. I was confused. And I said things I shouldn't have when we were at the dance."

"So, you thought I was the bad guy?"

"Sort of. It was a misunderstanding, I admit. But the truth is that I had no right to put myself in the middle. That's not what a professional writer does."

"You're a great writer," Leo said and pulled out a crumpled sheet of paper and unfurled it. She recognized the writing as her own, as he flipped the page over.

"My fears," she said. "How did you—"

"I need to know why you decided to stay after seeing that our town wasn't what you expected in the first place."

America knew exactly why she had stayed, and it had little to do with her job. "I stayed because that first day when you brought me a tree and things to decorate it with, it felt like home. You felt like home in a way that I don't fully understand yet," America said and eyed the paper. "Where did you find that?"

"It was on the ground over there." Leo read the words she had scribbled, "I'm afraid I will never be a real writer, and more afraid that I'll leave Christmas Cove and never see Leo again after this assignment."

She took the paper, with its singed corners, and read her words again in her mind.

"Did you mean it?" he asked, with a tender note in his voice and a flex of his fingers where they wrapped around her hands.

America looked at him, though her brows scrunched in the middle and pulled at her cheeks. "Yes. I meant it all."

"And are you still afraid of that?" he said, pulling her closer to him. His heat radiated off him and his gaze pierced her. "The part about never seeing me again?"

"Yes. But the fear didn't burn in the fire like it was supposed to," she said.

Leo's fingers came to the side of her neck and played with the little curls, sending a shiver to her core. He pulled out his paper from that night, blackened from grazing the fire. "Mine didn't burn either."

Taking his paper in her hands, she unfolded it and read the words. "I'm afraid America will leave, and I'll never get the chance to tell her that I'm falling in love with her." America sucked in a breath.

"Apparently, we're both bad shots since we both missed the fire," he laughed.

America couldn't hold in her giggle for long, though it alternated with tears of joy. "You love me?" she asked between giggles.

He nodded and pulled her in close. "I love you, America Greene, and I never want to be parted from you from this day forward."

If a kiss could be a promise, this one was it. His lips pressed into hers as his hand cradled the back of her head. He touched her lips lightly at first and then deeper and with more power. Her eyes closed tightly, as though she could feel their passions uniting like when the sun plunges into the water on the horizon at sunset.

Leo pulled away, breathless, before opening his eyes again. His relaxed face lit up with a smile, though his brows formed that little U in the middle. She worried if the kiss had been bad. Or—she looked at his feet, thinking she'd stepped on his toes.

"I need to apologize to you, too," Leo said, and America listened, unsure of anything he had done that warranted an apology. "I'm sorry I got your hopes up about pulling off Christmas here in town. I was sort of carried away by your excitement. But in truth, when you offered to help decorate Main Street, I jumped at the chance to spend more time with you."

America felt a blush warm her cheeks. She had wanted to spend more time with him, and all along he was egging her forward so that he could be with her, too. "You're forgiven."

"Just like that?" he asked.

"Just like that." America nodded and bit back a giggle. He was so cute when he was vulnerable. "Don't you think it's funny that we both had the same idea to keep each other around?"

Leo laughed. "I don't suppose this means you can stay for a while. I'd really like to get to know you more and maybe go on another date."

"I think I can stay for a while." America took his hand and began up the shore towards the gravel path. "You know that Victorian on Main with the pink trim?"

"Manner Manor?"

"That's the one." she couldn't help but giggle again at the name. "Well . . . I bought it. It needs some renovations—or a lot of renovations—before I can move in, but I think it will be a fun project to do. There's a cute little room at the top of the stairs with a round ceiling that's going to become my office."

Leo pulled her to a stop and ceased her rambling. "You're moving here? For me?"

"Don't flatter yourself. I'm here for the watersports."

"What?" He chuckled.

As she looked over the rolling hills dotted with red barns and painted white steeples poking out above the naked tree line, she said, "I love this place. It's filled with hope and kindness. Even though it's missing its holiday traditions, those things are only an outward expression of what the town feels in its heart. In truth, it's the most Christmassy place I've ever been to."

"That's beautiful," Leo said and pulled her in close. "You're beautiful."

Their lips met again, and her butterflies returned with force. The kiss was quick, but good.

"What are we going to do about the incorporation?" America asked. "I don't think we are going to get enough people."

"One less to go now."

America held up three fingers. "My parents are moving here, too. I told them about it, and they wanted to come. Apparently, a week alone in Italy made it clear to them that they wanted out of the city and to be close to me. And since I'm living here now, so are they."

"That's amazing," he said. "They were very sweet when I met them a little while ago. They remind me of my mom and dad, actually. It's funny, seeing them in the cabin dancing around the kitchen, it was as though I was seeing my own parents. You're quite lucky that you have them."

"I know," she said.

"Did you finish your article?" he asked.

"Almost. I told my boss that the story isn't done yet, but I think I captured the essence of this place."

"I'm sure it will be great," he said with all the confidence of a New York Times Best-Selling Author.

"You don't know that," America said. "Just because your mother was a language arts teacher doesn't make you some sort of an expert."

He stood proud with his shoulders back and chin out. "Yes, it does."

Her giggle turned to guffaw at the way he responded so matter of fact. His banter was refreshing and smart. He would challenge her, and anticipation rose in her chest that she would get to take her time getting to know him and learn to play with him in her own way.

"Thank you for doing everything you could. It means more to me than I know how to say," Leo said. "One more thing. How did you find out it wasn't me who requested the article? And who did?"

"It was easy. I asked my assistant. Would you believe it was the mayor of Elizabethtown? Thorpe is his name," America said.

"Of course it was. That son of a . . ." Leo kicked rocks.

"When I discovered you were the mayor, I wrongly thought *you* had wanted me here to cover the Christmas festivities. It makes sense now that there was no Christmas waiting for me, since you hadn't wanted me here in the first place—"

"Believe me, I wanted you here," Leo said and bit his cheek on one side. "Do you know what he wanted, though?"

"I'm guessing it has to do with the incorporation. But I don't really know."

"I have an idea what he's on about," Leo said. "I'm sorry, I have to go. I have some business to get to before everything shuts down for Christmas Eve." Leo made for his truck and opened the driver's door. "Will you tell your parents thank you for the breakfast?"

"They made you breakfast?"

"It was good. Too bad you missed it. Where were you, anyway?"

"I went to see Carol. And my new house." Pride in her impulsive decision welled in her heart. "Now go." America shut the truck door and leaned in through the window. "I'll see you tomorrow."

# CHAPTER 33

Leo turned the key, and with some coaxing of the gas pedal, the engine rumbled to life. His truck pulled out of the driveway and onto the main road from town. The truck, weighed down with his heaps of questions for Mayor Thorpe, chugged steadily into Elizabethtown, where he pulled the tires up onto the sidewalk in front of the mayor's office.

A security guard yelled at him to move, but Leo ignored his protests when he got out, slammed the door, and ran inside the stately building.

"I need to see him," Leo said to the receptionist. The young woman's doe eyes and blank expression of shock softened him a bit, and he tried again with a smile. "Is the mayor in?"

"He's in a meeting, sir," she said and picked up the telephone receiver. She banged out a number, presumably the police, and shifted her eyes around the lobby to anywhere but Leo's face.

"Never mind," Leo said and turned as though he was going to leave, but then bolted down the hallway instead.

Although he hadn't been there in years, he still knew right where to go. This building was all polished marble and carved woodworking and moldings. The mayor's office had two wide French doors that spilled into its own vestibule where a fireplace once roared and served as the building's primary heat source.

Eyeing the doors, Leo let himself in and prepared to give the man a piece of his mind.

The mayor, startled by the sudden intrusion, dropped the call he had been on and stood back. Fear crossed the man's face with a combination of pinched brows and wide eyes. Leo recognized the expression and put his hands up in a non-threatening way.

"What are you doing here?" Mayor Thorpe demanded. "You can't just let yourself into my office."

"Nice to see you too, brother," Leo said and approached the man.

"Seriously, Leo, why are you here?"

"No 'how are you, I've missed you, good to see you'?" Leo said and put his arms out. "Come on, John."

John came around from the relative safety of the desk and met Leo with outstretched arms. They hugged, as brothers do, with three quick pats on the back and a slap up the back of John's head.

"I suppose I deserve that," John said. "Is this about the incorporation?"

"Yes, of course it is." Leo's temper reemerged at the smug way his brother said the words.

"Listen, the law is clear. There's nothing I can do about it. Your town is simply too small to take care of itself, and I have an obligation to help the citizens there. Just as you would have done for me, if the tables were turned. We didn't write the town's agreement, and we can't be mad at the fact that it's triggered now," John said and sat back at his desk chair.

The door opened and two police officers came in. "You want this man removed?"

Leo's heart thumped in his neck, and he tightened his hands around the wood arms of the chair. He searched his brother's expression for any indication of his fate.

John stood and smiled. "It's all right, boys. This is my brother. He won't hurt me, and he was just about to leave. Give us a couple minutes, will ya?"

The officers hesitated before they walked out and shut the door.

Out of immediate danger, Leo released his grip. "I understand it's not your fault, but I've filed an appeal with the county for a head count on Christmas Eve anyway. We're close, you see."

"How close?"

"A couple people. Maybe two or three."

"Is this even what you want?" John asked. "I mean, you can barely support yourselves over there as it is. You're only limping along and avoiding the inevitable here. Your town will eventually dry up, just like the lake. The cove is gone, and it's not coming back."

The thought of the town being gone forever felt like another death to him. He moved there and became mayor to keep that connection alive between him and his parents. If the town went away, he feared that the memory of his parents would be gone forever, too. Leo didn't want that to happen. He wanted his town to thrive. *He* wanted to thrive there, with a family of his own. With America.

It was her information about the mayor of Elizabethtown that clued him into his brother's scheming and was the sole reason he had dragged himself to John's doorstep now. "Did you request that magazine to do a feature about the Cove?"

"I did," John said plainly.

"Why would you do that? To embarrass me?"

"I knew the town was done for, and I figured some P.R. about the place would drive tourism to the area." A humorless smile broadened across John's face, and Leo had a mind to slap it off.

Whatever had amused John, Leo suspected he wouldn't like it much. "What's your angle? You always have an angle."

"I suppose you'll find out soon enough," John admitted. "There's a resort that wants to move into the area that borders our two towns. The owner will never get the permits from both of us, so the project is on hold for the time being."

"I don't follow. What does that have to do with the article?" Leo asked.

"It's simple. The article was meant to gain support for a revitalization of the area after the incorporation. I mean," he chuckled, "who doesn't like a good comeback story? Am I right?"

Leo stood, and the chair crashed backwards onto the floor. "You're betting against me? This isn't some kind of game. I love Christmas Cove. It's my home, John. You can't just do this!"

John scribbled something on a paper and trained his gaze downward. "Yes, I can, Leopold. You've left me no other choice."

"Is this why you moved here? To humiliate me and take over my town?" Leo barked.

John paused and gently placed the pen on the desk. He looked up with buried sadness in his eyes. "I moved here for the same reason you did. Only you got to the area first, and we both know that one town isn't big enough for the both of us. Wouldn't you agree?"

"I would," Leo said, though it pained him when his brother was right.

"To be honest, you got the better town. Until that dam broke, and the cove dried up, you had what I wanted. Sometimes, the chips fall the way they will, and there's nothing anyone can do about it."

"I suppose not. It wasn't your fault that the storm hit." Leo walked to the door, having nothing else to say to his brother.

"And look at it like this, once our two towns are united, we can bring in that resort. Think about all the jobs and opportunities we'll have—"

Leo stopped him. "*If* our towns unite."

John put his hands up in surrender. "Fine, Leopold. You have your little head count, and we will see who comes out on top. But I'm telling you, this is going to be a good thing. Trust me."

Trust was something Leo had in short supply when it came to matters of his brother. He refused to look back as he exited. "Merry Christmas, John." Leo slammed the door behind himself and took a deep breath.

With as much dignity as he could muster, Leo walked down the hall. A smile hid his anger as he passed by the receptionist. Outside, he apologized to the guard and made his way to his truck before someone had a mind to tow the thing.

There was only one place he wanted to be, in Christmas Cove, with the people he loved and cared about. The head count was his last hope to save the Cove. Regret stung with every inhale of cold air that filled his chest. He wished he had done more while he had the chance. Leo wouldn't make that mistake again.

# CHAPTER 34

"THANK YOU SO MUCH, MR. JANOWITZ, AND MERRY Christmas." America stared at the screen on her phone in disbelief as it went dark.

"Who was that on the phone?" her mother asked.

"My boss. He just offered me my own column in the magazine. It's the most wonderful Christmas present." She dropped her phone on the counter and looked out the window, hoping to see Leo's red truck coming. There was no one else she wanted to share the news with at that moment.

"That's tremendous," her father said and gave her a side hug.

"I sent in my updated story yesterday afternoon after Leo and I talked. It went live at midnight. Mr. Janowitz said my article already has more social media shares than any other story in its first day, except the one about the ice castle last year. It was really good. I edited it and . . ." America shook the tangent from her head. "I digress. He wants me to be a Senior Special Interest Writer and cover something like Christmas Cove for each issue." America caught a glimpse of her face in the window reflection. She looked simultaneously excited and terrified. "I can't believe it."

America's mom hugged her tightly. "We are enormously proud of you. But will you be able to write from here? You just moved here, so I hope so."

"It's not a problem at all. Several of Jet Trek's writers work from various locations around the globe." America looked up at the road again, but there was no red truck in sight. "He should be here by now."

Just as she was giving up on getting to town in time for the count, jingling bells rang through the air. She spun and saw Leo in a carriage, with his trusty steed, approaching the cabin. She clapped her hands together at the treat coming her way. "Bingo's here."

"What is he doing?" her mom asked.

"Trying to impress you," America quipped back.

Sandwiched between her parents' shoulders, they crowded into the window and watched Leo pull the reins and tie up the horse on the front porch banister. Her father nudged her towards her mother, and she nudged back the other way. America felt like she was in a pinball machine and laughed.

"I don't think he's trying to impress me or your mom. He's trying to impress you," her dad teased. "By the look in your eyes, I'd say it's working, too."

Leo waved at them standing in the window and they all jumped backwards in unison. Her mother flung one drape, and her father flung the other to where they met in the middle. It was far too dramatic for the occasion, and their silliness was one of the things she loved most about her parents. They knew how to have fun.

Leo knocked on the cabin door, and America put her hand on the handle. "Who is it?" she asked, knowing full well that Leo was there.

"Housekeeping," he joked in a high-pitched voice.

"I didn't order room service," she said back.

"But did you order a ride to town?" Through the peephole she saw a wide grin and a small shake of his head, which caused her to suck in a laugh.

America opened the door and gestured for him to enter. "You're late."

"My copilot was wary about the cold. I had to warm his blanket before he would leave the barn." Leo pointed over his shoulder with his thumb. "Prima donna."

"Indeed," America said. "You know my parents?"

"Nice to see you again, Mrs. Greene." He shook her mother's hand. "Mr. Greene."

"You can call me Vi," her mother said.

"And you can call me Paul. And it's good to see you again so soon," her dad said. "America tells us that you two worked out some things?"

"We did," Leo said. "You have a very special daughter."

America felt his fingers brush against hers, and she intertwined hers with his. It was the first time they had properly held hands, not to help her up or stop her from slipping on ice. It felt good and right, and she squeezed a little tighter.

"We think so too," her dad said and smiled at Leo as though giving him approval. It was a small gesture, but she knew it had weight.

"Are you ready to go, then?" Leo asked. "Can I help you with your coat?"

America plucked her coat from the hook by the door and handed it to him, Leo slid her favorite red puffer up her arms and positioned the shoulders. She turned and mouthed a thank-you to him while she zipped and snapped the closure. While she dug in the pockets for her gloves, Leo wrapped a fluffy white scarf around her neck.

The ride into town, though beautiful, was spectacularly

chilly. An open-air carriage wasn't as romantic as it could have been when she was shivering and having to listen to her mother point out every bird, branch, and barn that they passed from the cabin all the way to Main Street.

"Forgive my mother. She doesn't get out much," America said, and everyone laughed as they turned onto Main.

The street was more dazzling than the last time she had seen it at night. Twinkling mini-lights hung from all corners of the buildings and across the road in a few places, and trees were lit in just about every window. On the Manner Manor's front door, someone, probably Carol, had hung a wreath with a big red velvet bow at the top.

America pointed as they passed by. She hadn't even moved in yet and the place already seemed like home. She would have much to do before next Christmas to get the place ready for a grand holiday party she planned to throw. No matter the outcome of the count, she wasn't going to let Christmas go.

People, some she recognized, others she hadn't seen before, strolled the streets and ducked into the couple of open businesses for some last-minute shopping or cups of hot cocoa. There appeared to be far more than the hundred-fifty residents required to stave off the acquisition of the town, though they wouldn't know for sure until the count was complete.

"Do you think we'll have it?" she said with hope dripping off her lips. "I mean, look at all these people."

"I have a good feeling, but let's not jinx anything," Leo said as the carriage stopped in front of the plaza at Town Hall.

Looking back down the street, America noticed Carol and Edwin walking together towards the fountain where the count was to take place any minute. "Will you look at that? Miracles *are* possible," America said.

"No matter what happens next," Leo jumped down and tied the reins. "Look at what we've accomplished here. The town is alive again."

Leo was right. She may have started things off, with the help of Pa, and Carol, and Leo, but the town had run with it. Leo helped her down from the carriage, and she snuggled into his embrace as they took in the happy scene. It was better than any Christmas card. It was real.

"I'm thankful for you," Leo said. "You brought joy back into the town. When you accused me of not doing more for the Cove, I got so mad because you struck at the truth. I had given up just like everyone else. But look at all this. Imagine what we can do as a community if we all want it enough."

"I think everyone did want it, but were too scared. You just needed some fresh air," America said and craned up for a kiss on his cheek.

He turned his head and caught the edge of her mouth, and she threw her arms around him. Their hug was warm. And short.

"Ahem." A man cleared his throat. "Are you Leopold Thorpe, mayor of Christmas Cove?"

"That's me," Leo said.

"Thorpe?" America whispered.

"Brothers," Leo whispered back. "Later."

The man outstretched his hand to Leo. "The name's William Doyle. I'm the lawyer representing the state. Is everyone assembled for the official head count?"

Leo looked around and nodded his head. "It's now or never," he spoke to himself, though America heard. He walked up the steps to the Christmas tree. Backlit by the tiny lights, Leo put his hands up to hush the crowd. When he had the people's attention, he announced the count. "Good evening, Christmas Cove!"

The crowd applauded, and a very real electricity traveled

through the air. It was probably the most exciting thing to happen in the Cove in years. America put her arms around her parents' waists and waited for Leo to speak again.

"I need everyone to group into sets of ten people for the count," he said. "From left to right, the first ten huddle together and then so on. Mr. Doyle is going to check each group, and we will have the official numbers in a few minutes. I thank you all for coming out here on this rather chilly Christmas Eve night. Now, go ahead and split up."

Leo stayed on the steps for the duration of the count, and when the groups finished sorting themselves out, he motioned for the lawyer to begin. Mr. Doyle started with America's grouping, counting to ten and then moving to the next. She watched as he made his way clear across to the other side of the plaza before joining Leo back on the steps beside the Christmas tree that they had all helped decorate.

They stood in each other's confidence for a moment, and then she saw it. Leo's face lost all color and his life seemed to leave his cheeks. It was unwelcome news. Her eyes scanned the groups quickly. She knew the count would be close. Two or three under, but as she counted the sets of friends, family, and neighbors, she saw they had come up shorter than she had predicted.

Leo took a step forward. The lawyer joined him at his side and spoke to the residents. "I'm so sorry, but Christmas Cove simply doesn't have the numbers. I wish I could deliver better news to you tonight, it being Christmas Eve and all. There are some legalities to work out in the new year, but please know that the city of Elizabethtown has your best interests at heart. Some good news: The mayor of Elizabethtown has assured me there are no plans to rename Christmas Cove. It will now simply be a neighborhood of Elizabethtown."

As the people spoke to one another in a hum, America

walked towards Leo, and they met at the fountain. She gave him a hug, as though that could fix his disappointment, and held him while the shock washed over him.

"I really thought we had it, America," Leo said.

"We do have it." She took his face in her gloved hands. "Look at all these people. Look at this tree, the decorations, the smiling faces. Christmas isn't a place, it's something that lives in all of our hearts. Don't forget why you came back here after your parents passed away. Because it felt like home to you, and it always will."

"Yeah," Edwin said as he slapped Leo on the back. "Who cares if you're not mayor anymore? That just means more free time to do other things. Like cleaning up the mess you left in the stable."

"Or helping me renovate that house down there," America said, pointing down the street.

"Or fixing that dock of yours," Carol added. "What? You never know when you might need it."

Leo shook his head at Carol. "Never," he said.

She grinned. "One can hope."

"How many did we need?" Edwin said.

Leo held up two fingers. "Just as I thought. And I made certain to include the Townsends in the count. We still didn't have the numbers."

Edwin patted Leo on the shoulders. "It's all right. I'm dang proud of you for what you've done, with the help of the lovely Miss Greene, over the past couple of weeks. And I'm glad you two worked things out. Love will make you do crazy stuff."

America threw her head back. "Does everyone know?"

"What, that you two lovebirds are meant to be together?" her dad said. "Yes. We all know."

America had no choice but to laugh it off. Sometimes it's hard to see what is true and good because it hides behind fear. She remembered the paper that had failed to burn up in the bonfire, and the fear that she would never see Leo again. "Leo, do you still have the little papers?"

"Yeah, why?" He pulled out a small wooden box and handed it to America. "What you're looking for is in here."

Her brows scrunched together. *Why would my fear be in a box?* She wondered.

The clock tower on the old church began to mark the hour. "Listen to those bells. It's midnight, which means it's Christmas," she said, smiling, and looked up to the sky. "And it's snowing." Emotions flooded into the back of her misty eyes as tiny flakes dusted her lashes.

Leo kissed her cheek. "Go on, open it."

With shaky hands, she opened the wooden lid and saw the most beautiful snowflake she had ever seen. When her eyes finally left the glittering ring and met Leo's gaze, he bent down onto one knee. She gasped.

"You never have to fear losing me ever again. I love you, America Greene. I meant what I said yesterday about not wanting to spend another day without you in my life." He smiled and took a deep breath before continuing. "I love that you love Christmas as much as you do. I love that you laugh with me. I love how caring you are and how you want others to be happy and whole. You embody that kind of love that I so admired about my own parents and never thought I would have for myself. I don't deserve you. But I hope you'll have me."

Stunned didn't quite cover it, but America felt her heart would burst if she didn't kiss the man that instant. There was no hesitation in her answer, her heart had already made its decision the moment he brought that dinky Christmas tree to the cabin the morning when she planned to head back to the city. He was everything she wasn't looking for, but everything she needed. He was her Christmas.

"Yes. A thousand times, yes," she said as she kneeled down to kiss him. "Merry Christmas, Leo Thorpe."

The clapping and cheering of over a hundred people gathered around them in the plaza drowned out the drumming of her heart. America hadn't realized they were on display until that moment, but nothing felt wrong about holding the man she loved in her arms and falling into his. This was the scene she had dreamed about being included in her favorite book, but it was now hers alone to relish forever.

"Merry Christmas, America."

# EPILOGUE

AMERICA HIT SEND ON HER EMAIL AND CLOSED HER LAPTOP. She sat back in her rattan chair, surrounded in her office by her plant babies. Succulents and rich palms lined every horizontal surface between the stacks of books she had been collecting over the summer.

In her city apartment, there wasn't much room for books. But since renovating the office in her new house, she had made it a priority to surround herself, and fill the bookcases, with as much inspiration as she could find.

The white sheer drapes fluttered into the room on the autumn breeze that smelled of apples and pine. She had grown to love this time of year in the country when the thick musk of summer gives way to a cool crispness in the air. When anticipation rustles in the red and yellow leaves shaking off the past and preparing for a season of renewal and rebirth of a new year.

Footfalls behind her tore her from her daydream. A steaming mug appeared over her head and down to the desktop. Leo leaned over her shoulder and kissed her cheek. "Done with your story?"

"Just sent it off. I can't believe I've already done three features this year. Being a full-time writer is exactly what I'm made for."

"I'm really proud of you for taking the leap into this. I know it was scary at first, transitioning from editor to writer, but you've done it with such grace and enthusiasm. And had time to put up with me this entire year," Leo said.

"I didn't put up with you, you just always hang around, like a cat," she said and took a sip of the coffee.

"Or like your little friend there?" Leo pointed at the tree outside the window.

"My squirrel?" America asked with a grin pulling on her cheeks. "I suppose you're like Bobby, a little bit. He's cute. You're cute. He watches me while I work. You watch the news while I work. He likes to eat food. You like to eat food."

"He wouldn't know what to do without you," Leo said. "And I wouldn't know what to do without you in my life, either."

"Nor would I, Leopold."

Leo kissed her nose the way she liked. It was a prelude to an inevitable kiss on the lips and a cradling of her head or face in his hand, and he did not disappoint.

"Dinner?" he asked as he pulled away.

She took his hand, and they walked down the stairs together. "I was thinking about the wedding . . ."

"Food first," Leo chuckled. "Then wedding talk."

# PLEASE REVIEW

We hope you enjoyed *Christmas Cove* by Sarah Dressler. If you did, we would ask that you please rate and review this title. Every review helps our authors.

Rate and Review: Christmas Cove

# MEET THE AUTHOR

Sarah Dressler, originally from Florida, now calls the mountains of Colorado home. Beginning her writing career as an award winning fashion blogger, Sarah now writes fiction full time. She has spent her life traveling the world, first as the daughter of a US Air Force officer, and later as a military spouse. She enjoys sunset walks with her husband of nearly twenty years, and raising two very busy teenagers.

# OTHER TITLES FROM

## 5 PRINCE PUBLISHING